John Ruskin

**A Knight's Faith**

Volume 4

John Ruskin

**A Knight's Faith**
*Volume 4*

ISBN/EAN: 9783337285913

Printed in Europe, USA, Canada, Australia, Japan

Cover: Foto ©Andreas Hilbeck / pixelio.de

More available books at **www.hansebooks.com**

# BIBLIOTHECA PASTORUM.

## VOL. IV.

## A KNIGHT'S FAITH.

### PASSAGES IN THE LIFE OF SIR HERBERT EDWARDES.

COLLATED BY

## John Ruskin,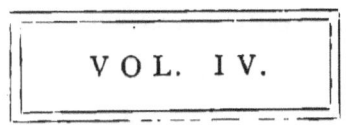

HONORARY STUDENT OF CHRIST CHURCH,
AND HONORARY FELLOW OF CORPUS CHRISTI COLLEGE, OXFORD.

GEORGE ALLEN,
SUNNYSIDE, ORPINGTON, KENT.
1885.

# PREFACE.

THE following pages are in substance little more than grouped extracts of some deeply interesting passages in the narrative published by Sir Herbert Edwardes, in 1851, of his military operations in the Punjaub during the winter of 1848-9.

The vital significance of that campaign was not felt at the time by the British public, nor was the character of the commanding officer rightly understood. This was partly in consequence of his being compelled to encumber his accounts of real facts by extracts from official documents ; and partly because his diary could not, in the time at his disposal, be reduced to a clearly arranged and easily intelligible narrative. My own abstract of it, made originally for private reference, had reduced the events preceding the battle of Kineyree within the compass of an ordinary lecture, which was given here at Coniston in the winter of 1883 ; but in preparing this for publication, it seemed to me that in our present relations with Afghanistan, the reader might wish to hear the story in fuller detail, and might perhaps learn some things from it not to his hurt.

My work at Oxford this last spring, and illness during the summer, prevented the final revision of the proofs; but here at last is the first of the three proposed sections, and I think there is every hope of the volume being completed by Christmas.

I have only to add that, although I have been happy in the friendship both of Sir Herbert and Lady Edwardes, my republication of this piece of military history is not in the least a matter of personal feeling with me;—it is done simply because I know it to be good for the British public to learn, and to remember, how a decisive soldier and benevolent governor can win the affection of the wildest races, subdue the treachery of the basest, and bind the anarchy of dissolute nations,—not with walls of fort or prison, but with the living roots of Justice and Love.

# CONTENTS.

# CONTENTS OF PART II.

# CONTENTS OF PART III.

# A KNIGHT'S FAITH.

## PART I.

### THE VALLEY OF FOUR HUNDRED FORTS.

### CHAPTER I.

#### *INTRODUCTORY.*

M Y friends of the North Countrie, it cannot but have seemed strange to you that I chose the story of a battle fought in India forty years ago, to be told you for your help in keeping your Christmas merry and holy in Coniston to-day. But this battle is singular in having been fought under the command of a Christian missionary, or modern military Bishop, differing from the military ecclesiastics of former ages, in that they, officially bishops, were practically soldiers; but the hero of this, my Christmas tale, officially a soldier, was practically a bishop.

Practically, indeed, both; and perfectly both:

I

a first-rate fighter of men, in war ; a first-rate
fisher of men, in peace : a captain whom all were
proud to follow ; a prelate whom all were eager
to obey,—and in a word, " a man under authority,
having soldiers under him," of whom his Master
might perhaps, in our days also, have said, " I have
not found so great faith, no, not in Israel."

What faith *does* remain vital, in modern spiri-
tual Israel, I neither recognise nor guess ; but
among the lives of men known to me, there is
not such another course of unflinching, straight-
forward, childlike belief in Heaven's will and help,
since—since I don't know when ! I really remember nobody quite like him—since St. Martin of
Tours ! *

You will have noticed that the battle was fought
on Waterloo day. It is very singularly also, in
the course of it, a miniature Waterloo, won by
sustaining for many hours the attack of a superior
force, till the time of retaliate charge arrived : but
it differed essentially from Waterloo, in that it
was won with native, not British troops : won with
a motley gathering of various tribes, some hostile

---

* This was written in 1883, when I had heard nothing of General
Gordon. But Gordon, Havelock, and Stonewall Jackson were all men
of Herbert Edwardes' stamp, only there is a vein of gaiety and natural
humour in Edwardes which makes him like St. Martin of Tours, in
a sense the others were not.

to each other, some on the eve of revolt to the enemy—not a single British soldier nor officer on the ground but the one in command, and the handful of faithful troops with which he wrought the victory, attached to him only by personal regard, by their knowledge of his justice, their experience of his kindness,* and the fidelity which over all the earth binds together the hearts of its brave and good men.

And I have therefore asked you to hear the story of it to-day, not that we may learn how battles may be won,—we find out usually, with less or more of blunder, how to do that;—but that we may learn the happier lesson how *men* may be won: what affection there is to be had for the asking; what truth for the trusting; what perennial honour for a moment's justice ; what lifelong service for a word of love.

My first business must be to give you the clearest outline possible in the time, of the events which led to the struggle ; and, before I can relate them, we must have distinct conception of the places in which they happened. Now, since it's Christmas time, will you pardon my having prepared this

---

* " And sympathy,"—adds Lady Edwardes, with significance : for without sympathy, in the high sense of intellectual penetration, kindness may be only folly, and intended aid, oppression.

lecture rather for young people, who don't always know everything they ought to know, than for the old ones, who always do. Of course, we old people know perfectly well that India is the little country that John Bull carries in his left-hand waistcoat pocket, with Canada and a few more miscellaneous articles in the pocket on the other side ; but for the children's sake, it is just as well that we should spare a minute or two now to look at a map or two. You know maps are, of course, in modern days, extremely scientific; but when drawn with contracting meridians, as the countries take violently different forms in their different groups, they are puzzling for young people, besides being apt to make them think *they*, too, may draw a country of one shape one day, and another the next. But these maps of mine are done in a much safer and pleasanter way. You put an ideal pin right into the middle of the country first, and pin it well down ; then you change yourself into a pelican, or a phœnix, or a frigate bird, or something of that sort, and you fly up above the pin in the middle of the country as high as ever you can, till you can see the country's edges all round, quite easily ; then you cry down to some bird of sense below to draw a cross through the pin—north and south, and east and west—till the ends of the cross come to the edges of the country—and beyond, far enough to make all the four arms of the cross equal. Then you draw the country as you see it exactly, not squinting, nor stretched, one way or another ; and then you can enclose the whole cross and it in a square, which you can easily make of some accurately measured and easily remembered size, merely by giving the branches a little more or less margin. Here, you see, is the whole of India enclosed in a square every quarter of which is 15 degrees, or 900 geographical miles, in the side. That is something more than 1,000 English miles the side; and in a map of so large a country the distances drawn are, in proportion to the earth's roundness, greater as they are farther from the centre; so you may say, for our present purposes, roughly, a thousand miles square, or a million of square miles, each quarter. Half of this, however, is Indian ocean, and Cachemire highland. India herself has not more than a couple of millions of square miles to reign over, and two millions of square miles may be easily said ; but if you like to cut the British islands out of another map on the same scale, and pin *them* down in the middle of India, thus, —you see the latter country isn't quite so easily carried in our waistcoat pocket.

One other principle I wish you to note in this
school map-making.  I always take my north and
south line through the capital, if central enough ;
otherwise, through any chief feature of the country,
natural or historical:—thus, for England and Wales
I take it through Holy Island, with the east and
west line through Lichfield.    But India is an easy
and perfect example ; for, taking the north and
south line through her capital, Delhi, it passes also
through her southernmost point, Cape Comorin,
and forms a measure for nearly all her length of
latitude.    I don't in the least know what Comorin
means, though it is Indian for something, certainly ;
but you can easily recollect it by remembering
that we English are making, or want to make,
a home of India now, instead of a mere inn or
caravanserai ; and so you can make a nursery
rhyme of it, saying—

> " Whether as a home, or inn,
>     Don't forget Cape Comorin."

On this map I have only marked the Indian
capital, and four Colony-capitals, Bombay, Seringa-
patam, Madras, and Calcutta, without their names,
for then the children will see exactly where they
are : whereas if you put the name, the child never
can tell at which end of it the town is.    I know
that, by experience, because in the first map I

made for my father to travel by, when I was a little boy, I copied all the names in their proper places, with extreme care, but put the towns under their names or above, or at this end or that of them, as looked neatest ; and as the postillions had no knowledge of these arrangements, my father was obliged to take to his vulgar road map again. Also, when you don't write the names, the children have to write them in their own minds, which is far better for them.

In the north of this great peninsula I draw, in dark blue, the courses of the main streams of the two great rivers, Indus and Ganges, with the four upper branches of Indus, of which the principal one, the Hydaspes, is that which gives Milton his grand line—

"Of Ganges or Hydaspes,—Indian streams,"

and is the one beside which we have presently to be patient. That, as well as the outer Hyphasis or Sutlej, is an Indian stream wholly; but the great Indus is half Cashmerian, longer than the Ganges, and though nothing like the biggest, the most important river in the world.

For, first, note of it that it cuts the highest mountain chain in the world in two. Neither Amazon nor Orinoco divides the Andes, nor Rhine nor Danube the Alps.* But the Indus cuts through the Himalaya.

Then, secondly, it not only divides the highest mountains in the world, but the World itself. The *old* world, that is to say, the only one hitherto worth thinking about,—though the Americans are now beginning to make themselves an appreciable quantity in animated nature. † But taking this side of the globe as, in the past, containing the total power of mortality, the Indus divides *it* into east and west. Whatever is west of Indus is

---

* A casual reader asks me why I don't name the Mississippi? Because I've no idea about the Mississippi, except as the drainage of a big swamp full of alligators. I may be wrong in this impression, but can't rectify it in correcting press. I've looked at Johnson's 'Atlas of the World,' Edinburgh, 1883 ; but the Mississippi is jammed into the chink of the map No. 30, which won't open, and it seems to join on to the Ottawa and Toronto railroad, which looks like another big river running into the St. Lawrence, so I've given it up.

† I meant the colonist Americans, of course ; for the old red ones I have the deepest respect,—and the white ones, who live enough or travel enough in Europe, become extremely nice ; witness Mr. Lowell and Mr. C. E. Norton, and Miss Alexander—extremely appreciable quantities all ;—but I trust that Miss Alexander will forgive my quoting, in my love of the Aborigines, the following passage of a letter received from her this morning (20th February, 1885), as I correct this slip of type.

"And I want to tell you, once for all, that my eyes are among the principal earthly blessings which I have to be thankful for. I am very far-sighted, and at the same time see near things very minutely, and can do the finest work, just as near-sighted people do. I never knew that other people did not see so plainly at a distance

Abrahamic, and progressive, like a tree ; whatever
is east of Indus, Brahmic, and, somehow or other,
evaporating into air, or crystallized into changeless
shape, like a jewel : so that from the birth of Christ,
since the Mahometans acknowledge Him as a
prophet, you may broadly say the world is Christian
and Brahmic. And between these it is not the
Bosphorus that bars,—the Bosphorus has no more
to do with the matter than the English Channel
—not so much, indeed, for English Breton and
French Breton are far more distinct people than

as I did, until one day, years ago, when we were living at Bellos-
guardo ; I was standing on the balcony, with some friends, when
one of them asked me what o'clock it was. I looked, as my habit
was, at the clock on Palazzo Vecchio, and answered : 'A quarter
past five.' 'But I wanted you to look at the clock !' said the other.
'I *am* looking at it,' said I. And then they all were astonished,
and said that it was impossible to see anything at that distance, and
would not believe that I could tell the time by that clock, until
they had found a watch somewhere, which exactly agreed with what
I said. The clock was, I think, about two miles away. But all
my senses are exceedingly acute, like those of our American Indians ;
and if I must tell you all the truth, there is an old story in the
family (who were among the first settlers of Connecticut), that my
grandfather's grandmother was an Indian. The family all laugh at
it, but I am much inclined to believe it, as it accounts, not only for
this physical peculiarity, but for the fact that I have never been able
really to like civilization, and feel always happier and more at home
in the woods than anywhere else. And if I appear to you sometimes 'vindictive,' you see that I come by it honestly."

(N.B.—This charge was in consequence of some of the young lady's
expressions about vivisectionists, and what she would like to do to
them, in a former letter.—J. R.)

Attic and Ionian Greek ; but the *Indus* is the river of Separation.* West of *that*, all civilized nations believe either in the God of Isaac or of Ishmael,—to the north are Sarah and the children of the free woman,—to the south, Hagar and the children of the bond woman ; but all having Abraham to their Father, and believing in one Father-God, Jehovah, Jove, or Allah. But east of Indus you have the numberless Brahmic—there is no other so good general epithet—re-

* *Note by Lady Edwardes.*—The people of the Punjáb belong to the great Aryan family. A large proportion of the dwellers in the five " Doábs " (the natural divisions formed by the rivers of the Punjáb proper) are Játs, supposed to be the same as the Scythian Getes of classical authors. Recent investigations point to the Játs as the real forefathers of the wandering gipsies of Europe (*Edinburgh Review*, July, 1878). The Indus divides the languages.

The history of the Punjáb is the history of successive conquests. On the banks of its rivers first settled the Aryan invaders of India, some two thousand years before Christ ; and here were, probably, composed the Vedic hymns which, in the nineteenth century. are studied with such deep interest. The India mentioned by Herodotus, as subjugated by Darius Hystaspes, about 500 B.C.. probably means only the Punjáb.

Our earliest information concerning the country is derived from the accounts by Diodorus Siculus, and Arian, of the campaigns of Alexander the Great. The Macedonian conqueror crossed the Indus about 327 B.C., probably by a bridge of boats at Attock.

His great victory over Porus was fought on the east bank of the Jhelum ; and when farther advance was prevented by the discontent of the troops, they were conveyed down the five rivers in ships by Near-chus. Mahometanism arose in the seventh century, and after three hundred years of resistance the Hindûs were conquered by Mahmoud, of Ghuznee, about A.D. 1000.

ligions, Hindū, Chinese, Tartar, Japanese, and what not, attaching themselves no more to any one conceivable or visible God, but floating and whirling round any quantity of inconceivable, invisible, and in their symbols, monstrous gods,— gods like cuttle-fish, with uncountable legs ; gods like cauliflowers, with inseparably sprouting heads ; orbicular gods, with no ends ; polygonal gods, with any quantity of ends ; air gods, water gods, mud gods, vacuum gods, infinitely ugly abortions of things without origin, infinitely shapeless odd-lings of unhatchable egg.

Now, *this* is separation indeed !—and note with what strange decision, on this and on that side of the river, the bounding line is drawn. On the one side, the Hindūs have a sacred tradition that they must not pass it ; on the other, the Greek power is for ever stayed by it. Alexander, by the hindmost branch of it, conquers Porus, but buries Bucephalus, and eastward he rides no more.* But a wilder power than the Greeks is stayed by

---

* During the second Cabul campaign the monument erected by Alexander over his favourite horse, Bucephalus, was passed by the British army in nearly as perfect a state as the day when it was erected, and Greek coins were found on the spot. These ancient " mounds " are frequently found in different parts of these wild frontier lands, and trace the course of this great warrior of old. Some of the pieces of ancient stone-carving found, distinctly show the mingling

the Indus also. You see this central mountain, gathering into a knot the chain of hills on its western bank. That is called 'Solomon's Throne' to this day, and it is the term of the *Arabian* power. The miraculous strength of the Ishmaelite, which swept round seven thousand miles of the earth, resting westward on Granada in Spain, and centralised in the Arabian peninsula, founded the thrones of his caliphs by the Persian Gulf, and planted its last standard on this mountain, the Throne of Solomon, above Indus' shore. Put your terrestrial globe with the Indus under the brass meridian, and west of it you have seven thousand miles of Mahometans : east of it, seven thousand miles of Indians ; but, strangely, close to the river, within the very sound of cannon shot from side to side, are two types of the evermore divided races, each among the most perfect that, in this century, exist—the Sikh and the Afghan.

I told you just now that I drew the meridian of my map of India through Delhi, as the capital of India. Religiously, it is the capital of all the East, and is to Indian faith what Rome is to Christian. But, encompassed by the loop of the

of the stiff figures of Indian sculpture with the more graceful lines of Grecian art. (See ' A Year in the Punjab,' vol. i., pp. 340, 341, 342, for further Greek illustrations.)

northern Himalaya, in the plain, so called, of the Five Waters, the tributaries of Indus,* has arisen within the last four hundred years, a kingdom of a strange sort of evangelical Hindūs, who believe in a Divine Book, instead of Brahma (and get leave in their Book to do pretty much what they like), a practically strong and prosaic race, Hindū Round-heads and Independents, as it were, who yet have a trace of old imagination in their hearts, and adore an Elysian island in a ' Lake of Immortality,' actually visible and visitable somewhere ; who also are the most military race of Hindostan, and to whom all her national enthusiasm looked, says Sir Herbert Edwardes, for the expulsion of Christianity from the Peninsula. After forty years' gathering of strength, under Runjeet Singh, the Sikh army, that is to say the Sikh nation, (for every Sikh is a soldier,)† challenged us to fight for the Indian Empire, " and was humbled to the dust in a

---

\* More properly. the Indus with its four tributaries, being—

    The Jehlum, ancient Hydaspes.

    The Sutlej, ancient Hyphasis.

    The Chenāb, ancient Acesines.

    The Ravee, ancient Hydrastes.

† *Note by Lady Edwardes.*—After the Mahometan subjection of the Punjāb came the Sikh power, which was, in the first instance, a movement of religious reform among the Hindūs, begun by Nānuk in 1526, but was developed into a military commonwealth in 1675, under Nānuk's tenth successor in the leadership of the sect—named no

campaign of sixty days. In February, 1846, Lord Gough encamped his avenging army under the walls of Lahore. Duleep Singh, the boy-sovereign of the Punjāb, knelt to the Governor-General of India for forgiveness ; Lord Hardinge raised him from the ground, and reseated him on the Sikh throne, shorn though it was of its former splendour. In the ' Land of the Five Waters ' he was still king of four."

The struggle, note you, had been primarily one of *creeds* : the Sikhs fought, not so much against England as against Christianity ; and being, as I said, a sort of obstinately reformed and petulantly pious Hindūs, they hate with theologic—no less than national bitterness, more than the Christian

matter what—who said to his followers, " Hitherto you have been Sikhs (disciples) ; henceforth you shall be Singhs " (lions). This common-wealth was called Khâlso (pure), and the combination of ascetic and knightly tendencies in its warriors made them fierce and gloomy fanatics, a character fostered by the cruel persecutions they under-went, whenever the continued struggles between them and their Mahometan neighbours gave the latter the ascendency.

Their founder Nānuk had aimed at establishing a society that should attract both Moslems and Hindūs.

He taught that there is one God, the Creator of all things, perfect and eternal, but incomprehensible ; that the knowledge of God, and good deeds, together, would procure salvation ; that the souls of the dead might (as the Brahmins said) live in other bodies ; but that the righteous might (as the Moslems said) hope for a consciously happy existence at last.

English on the other side of the world, the Mahometan Afghans on the other side of the Indus.

And having, before they attacked us, already
habitually robbed, and partially subdued, the Afghan
provinces nearest them, and on their side of the
Himalaya — having overflowed the ridge from
Afghanistan proper,* the first thing the Sikhs
ask of the British Government when they have
got its support, is to help them to collect their
customary taxes from this outlying, and only
under compulsion tributary, Afghan tribe.

The British Government thinks itself bound to
do so, but at the same time to see that its new Sikh
protégés do their Afghan taxing moderately, and
civilly, and not by mere inroad and casual pillage.
It allows a Sikh army of 1,500 irregular horse, a
regiment of cavalry and five of infantry, with two
troops of artillery, to be sent into the province to
enforce fiscal arrangements; but it places over them,
as supreme controller of movement and operation,

---

* *Note by Lady Edwardes.*—The Sikh military power ultimately
became predominant in the Punjáb, and especially in the present
century, under Runjeet Singh, who, by birth a Jât, rose to be
supreme ruler of the country, and after the fall of Napoleon in
1815 engaged several French generals to organize his army, which
they did most effectively.

They were a warlike race, and every man a soldier; and this rendered
them the most formidable antagonists that had yet confronted the
power of England in India.

an English officer. Not an old officer, neither ;
on the contrary, still in the fire of youth—born
in Nov. 1819—totally inexperienced in war, not
heard of yet in council, uncompetitive in any
manner of examination, and in military rank, lieutenant only. But the man who appointed him,
Sir Henry Lawrence, knew his metal, and sent,
to control an army of the fiercest soldiers of
India, in their invasion of the wildest tribes of
Afghanistan, a single English youth,—Lieutenant
Herbert Edwardes.

You Englishmen of the moor and glen, who are
proud of your country and its laws, is not *this* a
wonderful Christmas tale for you ? An altogether
true one—of only seven-and-thirty years ago !—
think you it ought already to be forgotten ?

# CHAPTER II.

## *THE VALLEY IS RECONNOITRED.*

NOW, have you got the look of all this, and the gist of it, well into your heads? Here the Indus, virtually always, young or old, deep in defile, or wide wandering in the plain, always a wild and wilful mountain torrent, the grandest kind of river. On the west of it, seven thousand miles of Mahometans; on the east, innumerable miles of Hindūs; and, to make the contrast more glittering, almost the best types of the men of each religion close to each other, on the river's very banks, only the ten or fifteen miles of its waves to part them.

I will show you pictures of both.*

Here is, first, the Mahometan, Kowrah Khan, a chief of the lower Derajat, the bit of plain between the Indus and Solomon's Throne. I must partly anticipate events here, in order to give you an idea of the character of this good and faithful ally. Hyder Khan, his son, serving with a contingent of

* The reference was to the excellent drawings by Mr. Arthur Severn, from the plates given in Sir Herbert's book.

their tribe in that part of Sir Herbert's force which was lying detached in the north before the battle of Kineyree, under General Cortlandt, and recognizing the need of clearing Sir Herbert's rear with all speed, of all rebels west of Indus, asks leave of General Cortlandt to go ahead alone, raise his father's clan, the Khosuhs, and drive Longa Mull, a rebel chief, across the river.   Sir Herbert's diary proceeds thus :—

"General Cortlandt gave him permission, but thought so little of it, that he never mentioned it to me.   Hyder Khan made but one request to a Pathan friend—that if he fell in the fight, ' he would ask the Sahib to revenge his death '; then joined his father, Kowrah Khan, and the two raised their clan for a grand struggle against their enemies, who mustered 500 strong * round Longa Mull, in front of the fortress of Ghazee Khan.   The Khosuhs attacked in the last hour of the night, were repulsed more than once, and at last drew off till morning dawned, when Kowrah Khan thus addressed his son : ' Son, you were a fool to pledge the honour of your tribe in this matter, but, as you have done so, the pledge must be redeemed.'   Then, dismounting

* Force of the Khosuhs not told ; probably about the same.   Their contingent afterwards to Sir Herbert is 400, but Longa Mull had one gun and five field-pieces.

from his own horse, and drawing his sword, he called upon every true Khosuh to follow him on foot, and leave their horses for the enemy to fly on ! The clan obeyed, and their now united assault proved irresistible.

Thus was this noble soldier left master of the fort of Dera Ghazee Khan, and of forty large, masted boats, collected by Longa Mull, at Moolraj's orders, to enable the rebel army to cross the Indus.

For this timely service, very handsome dresses of honour were given to all the Khosuh chiefs ; letters were sent by both the Maharajah and the Resident, thanking Kowrah Khan and his son ; and the dearly-loved title of ‘ Ali Já,’ or ‘ Of high degree ! ’ was conferred upon them.

Proud of both what they had done and what they had won, they followed me afterwards ‘ to the wars,’ with four hundred horsemen of ‘their own tribe, and shared with me many months of exposure and hard fighting, without any other recompense than their food !

These, indeed, were not Kowrah Khan's first fields. He had in earlier years striven army to army with the great Nuwab of Bhawulpūr, and when defeated, had given his daughter to the conqueror in marriage, as a proud acknowledgment of submission.

I recal these anecdotes of Kowrah Khan, because

my memory dwells with admiration on his character :
so brave, so humble, so hot in fight, so cool in council,
so sober and dignified in triumph, so smooth-browed
and firm amid disaster ; a man at all times to be
relied on.

Nor is it the least pleasing recollection of him, that,
when danger and difficulty had passed away, peace
returned, and the State had no more need of volun-
teers, Lord Dalhousie, with a just and unforgetting
gratitude, which rulers do not always imitate, not only
confirmed Kowrah Khan in possession of a jageer
of one thousand rupees a-year, but extended it also
to the lifetime of his gallant son ; added a money
pension of twelve hundred rupees a-year to Kowrah
Khan, and *gave a garden at their native place to the
family for ever."**

This, then, was the kind of man Sir Herbert could
find for his help among the Afghans. The second
portrait I show you is of his Hindū ally, the
Prince (Nuwab) of Bhawulpūr ; faithful and well-
meaning, but not to be counted on for active co-
operation. You would probably think him, to look
at him, much the fiercer warrior of the two—
Kowrah Khan's most manifest characters being grace
and gentleness.

* Italics mine, that you may notice the reward which the good soldier
cares for. Not a place at court, but a garden in his village.

Knowing what can thus be made visible to you of the two races with whom he has to deal, you must next know something of the province which this English youth is sent to take order with. Take your map of the district of the Upper Indus alone, and you will see that there is an inlet of the great plain of the river running up into the mountains, and more or less locked in by lower spurs of them.* This valley is, roughly, about the size of Yorkshire, and it is watered by rivers of its own, which flow down into it from the hills, and never get out of it again, but use themselves quite up in making it pretty. And it is, besides, in the fruitfullest latitude of the world,—that of Christ's country. Solomon's Throne, a hundred miles south, is exactly in the latitude of Jerusalem ; this mountain valley has the climate of Lebanon and Damascus.

" In spring, it is a vegetable emerald, and in winter, its many-coloured harvests look as if Ceres had stumbled against the great Salt range and spilt half her cornucopia in this favoured vale."

With the just-quoted earnest praise of his Indian friend, and this pretty praise of his Indian province,

---

* Height of hills to south-east of Bunnoo wanted,—as, indeed, of the hills all round. Sir Herbert is horribly careless about his trigonometry, except when he's got a fort to build !

I begin our excerpts from Sir Herbert's own diary; arranged and completed by him in 1851, and published under the title of 'A Year on the Punjāb Frontier.' A book of most faithful and perfect history, supported by every necessary document, and one which should have its place in every English library,—but chiefly in our national and civic ones. More may be learned from it than from the newspapers of as many days as it has leaves ; and henceforward I use it for my total narrative, interpolating only such explanatory notes as these broken extracts may require for their connection.

Such being the soil and climate of the valley he has to deal with, he next describes its people.

"Although forming a distinct race in themselves, easily recognizable, at first sight, from any other tribe along the Indus, they are not of pure descent from any common stock, and able, like the neighbouring people, to trace their lineage back to the founder of the family ; but are descended from many different Afghan tribes, representing the ebb and flow of might, right, possession, and spoliation in a corner of the Cabul empire, whose remoteness and fertility offered to outlaws and vagabonds a secure asylum against both law and labour. The introduction of Indian cultivators from the Punjāb,

and the settlement of numerous low Hindūs in
the valley, from sheer love of money, and the hope
of peacefully plundering by trade their ignorant
Mahometan masters, have contributed, by inter-
marriage, slave-dealing, and vice, to complete the
mongrel character of the Bunnoo people. Every
stature, from that of the weak Indian to that of
the tall Doorânee ; every complexion, from the
ebony of Bengal to the rosy cheek of Cabul : every
dress, from the linen garments of the south to the
heavy goat-skin of the eternal snows, is to be
seen promiscuously among them, reduced only to
a harmonious whole by the neutral tint of universal
dirt. . .

Let the reader take this people, and arm them
to the teeth ; then, throwing them down into the
beautiful country I have described, bid them scram-
ble for its fat meads and fertilizing waters, its
fruits and flowers,—and he will have a good idea
of the state of landed property, and laws of tenure,
as I found them in 1847. Such, indeed, was the
total confusion of right, that, by way of gaining
for this community a new point of departure, and
starting fair on an era of law and order, Colonel
Lawrence was obliged to declare that five years'
possession should be considered a good title. . . .

Mr. Elphinstone, writing in 1808, says of the Bun-

noochees, that though 'without any common government,' they 'pay some regard to the King's authority,'
*i.e.* the King of Cabul.  From that date, the Cabul
empire grew rapidly weaker ; and in a few years the
capital was unable to send a force to collect tribute
from such a distant province as Bunnoo ; and without a force, no attention ·was paid to either royal
messengers or royal Purwannuhs.  Bunnoo became
independent of its own lawful sovereign.  About
1822, the far more odious power, which had risen
up on the opposite bank of the Indus, began its
attempts to include Bunnoo in the Sikh empire.  If
the Bunnoochees were unwilling to pay tribute to
Cabul, they were quite resolved not to pay it to
Lahore ; and through a quarter of a century, in the
face of armies and devastations, they succeeded in
maintaining their new-gained independence.  . . .

Owning no external allegiance, let us see what
internal government this impatient race submitted to :
In truth, none.  Freed from a king, they could not
agree upon a chief ; but every village threw a wall
around its limits, chose its own *Mullick* (master),
and went to war with all its neighbours.

A highly intelligent native named Agha Abbas,
of Shiraz, who was employed by the late Major R.
Leech to make a tour through parts of the Punjab
and Afghanistan, in the year 1837, reported that

there were 'full four hundred, if not five hundred, forts and villages in the district.' (A fort and a village in their language mean the same thing. There was not an open village in the country.) Ten years later, I sent a spy before me into Bunnoo to draw me a rough map of it. He returned with a sheet of paper completely covered over with little squares and lozenges, and a name written in each, with no space between.

'Why, Nizamooddeen,' I said, 'what is this?'

'That,' he replied triumphantly, 'why, that's Bunnoo!'

'And what are all these squares?'

'Oh! those are the forts.'

A pleasing prospect for the individual to whom the subjugation of Bunnoo had been confided!"

Sir Herbert, then Lieutenant, Edwardes, received the charge in the middle of February, 1847. " From Lahore to Bunnoo was a month's march ; and the hot season of the Punjāb commences in March, and sets violently in in April. I had, therefore, at best a month allowed me to talk over an independent people, who had resisted Sikh supremacy for a quarter of a century ; and I think it is not very surprising that I signally failed in the attempt.

We entered Bunnoo on the 15th of March, and

were burnt out of it by the sun on the 1st of May. Of a lakh and three-quarters of rupees of revenue, due from the valley, we had collected only half a lakh ; and as to a peaceable settlement for the future (that is to say, an engagement, on the part of the people, to pay *anything* annually of their own free will), we had fully ascertained that it was hopeless.

Was, then, this first expedition fruitless ?

Far from it.   Two great objects had been gained.

Firstly.   A Sikh army, under the influence of a single British officer, had passed, unmolesting and unmolested, through a country, which before it never entered but to devastate, and never left but with heavy loss.

Secondly.   I had reconnoitred the whole valley, ascertained the strength of its tribes, and seen how both might be subdued.

Let me explain both these results.   The Sikh army was notorious for plunder ; and one of Colonel Lawrence's strictest injunctions to me at parting was: 'To make severe examples of every instance, and in very bad cases to send the offenders in irons to Lahore.'   For the first fortnight I had full employment.   On the line of march, in the morning, I did nothing but detect, stay, reprove, chase, overtake, and imprison plunderers, horse and foot ; and all the rest of the day my tent was besieged by the people of the country bewailing their damaged fields, and calling on me to punish the offenders.

Long indulged in military licence, the Sikh soldiers could not believe that they were no longer to be allowed to help themselves from every farmer's field, pull their firewood from every hedge, and drag a bed from under its slumbering owner, in order that they might take a nap on it themselves. The cavalry, too, thought it quite arbitrary that they should have to pay for the fodder of their horses (fine young corn, which the Zemindar intended one day to be bread !) But when the wholesome reform once dawned upon their convictions as a fact, and a few severe examples, before the whole force, showed what all plunderers had to expect, the men gave it up at once, and settled down into a completer state of discipline in this respect than is ever attainable in the camp of an Anglo-Indian army, where officers have no power of punishment on the spot. —(In the Company's army, there is nothing so difficult as to *convict* a native soldier of plundering ; or, if convicted by evidence, to get a sentence of punishment from the native officers who compose the court-martial. It would be a good thing, too, if the European officers would not consider themselves quite so much bound by *esprit de corps* to shelter their own men. It is a kindly, but mistaken, feeling.)

The news of the anti-plunder regulations in our camp spread through the country, and long preceded us to Bunnoo ; encouraging a third, at least, of the population to await our arrival in the valley, instead of flying bodily to the mountains as usual. Nor during our stay of six weeks in Bunnoo, were there more than two breaches of the new discipline. In the one case, some soldiers, by order of their officer (General Purtáb Singh), cut down a fine willow tree,* under whose shade the holy Syuds of a village were wont to sit and pray ; and I was induced, by the long services of the General, to let him off with compensation to the Syuds. In the other case, another holy man rushed into my tent, and complained that an elephant driver had begun to cut his green wheat, and carry it off as fodder for our elephants ; the Syud remonstrated in the only language he knew—viz., Pushtoo, and the Mahout replied with a still harder medium of communication. In proof of his story, the poor Syud was covered with blood. There being only four elephants in camp, a very short investigation brought the offence home to the servant of a Sikh chief, named Sirdar Soorjun Singh ; and I resolved to make a signal example of the depredator. A parade of the

* Not a willow really, but a pretty Indian tree like one, growing by stream-sides, for which I say ' willow ' as easiest English.

whole Sikh force was ordered ; the troops formed into a hollow square, and in spite of the personal entreaties of his master, the Mahout was tied up to the triangles and flogged—then passed with bare back down the ranks of his comrades. Assembling the officers, I then explained to them, and desired them to explain to their respective companies, that the people of the country, relying on my protection, had received us as friends ; but would resort to their old system of night attacks and assassinations, if the Sikh soldiers plundered them as of old ; that, consequently, the peace of the whole camp, and many men's lives, depended on the maintenance of discipline ; and so far as I was concerned, I would never overlook a breach of it.

After this there were no more complaints. Whether they paid revenue or not, the Bunnoochees flocked into our camp, and bought and sold with our soldiers, and sat and talked in our assemblies, as friends instead of enemies."

Sir Herbert was surely unjust to himself in saying above, p. 25, that his first effort at " talking over " the Bunnoochees had " signally failed." He has established pacific and intelligent relations between the Sikhs and their tributaries, —he has himself obtained the trust and respect of both ; and more than these, the courteous affection of all with whom he has had direct personal intercourse.

"The great question at issue between us—the Lahore tribute money—was referred to argument, instead of the sword; almost all the chiefs took heart, and returned from the mountains to join the national council in my tent, whether inclined to yield or determined to resist; their different characters were discriminated; many were won over to our side, and friendships formed which afterwards stood us in good stead. . .

One anecdote I must relate before leaving this subject, because it is most honourable to the Sikh force, and shows of what a high degree of discipline that military people is capable. Sikh detachments, and, indeed, all forces not at the capital (before Colonel Lawrence introduced regular pay), used to be paid by assignments on the provincial collectors of revenue; on whose solvency, or caprice, it depended how soon or how late they should realize their pay. The army sent to Bunnoo had a very worthless bit of paper indeed, drawn on one Dowlut Raie, the 'contractor' (and I may add, devastator) of several provinces on the right bank of the Indus. Either he could not, or he would not, honour it; and our poor fellows, obliged by me to pay ready money for everything they bought in the valley, were soon so distressed for food, that some of them dropped down under arms from weakness. Not till then was it reported to me by the officers, in their expressive language, that 'the whole force was hungry,' and wanted my permission to quarter on the enemy. They were, indeed, standing as sentries over the ripe corn-fields of the refractory Bunnoochees! I looked out from my tent, and saw the rich harvest of that prolific land, in every stage, from green to gold, waving temptingly around our camp; and thought discipline had for the nonce been most reverentially honoured! So I passed the word, for every soldier to cut enough food for himself and cattle for a fortnight; and in an hour, the harvest had vanished from those parts, as if locusts had passed over them. . . .

Thus, as I said before, was one great object gained by our otherwise unsuccessful expedition. The blood-thirsty and revengeful tribes of Bunnoo, and the army of their Sikh masters, had, for the first time, met in something resembling friendship; and parted again, without adding to the long account of mutual injuries and hatred. The small end of the wedge of civilized intercourse had at last been introduced."

Both as a farther illustration of the soldierly courtesy of Sikh character, and as a deeply interesting analysis by his friend and ally of Sir Herbert's own, the following farewell letter from the Sikh general, on the close of the first expedition to Bunnoo, though it is given by Sir Herbert only under the detached heading of "A Stray Recollection," deserves the reader's most attentive regard. The italics are all, of course, mine.

(After all his state titles, etc., etc.)

" My dear Friend,

" In a day or two we shall be at our journey's end ; and in the joy of returning home you will soon forget that you have been four months abroad. Sherbet, and ' beyd-mooshk,'* will drown the taste of the abominable waters of the Goombeeluh ; the clean streets of Lahore † will make amends for the watercourses and quagmires of Bunnoo ; you will have fireworks at night instead of attacks on the pickets ; the arrow of love instead of the spear of war ; and wanderings in the many-coloured garden,‡ instead of tiresome marches in the desert. How

---

* A perfumed beverage extracted from the willow, of which natives are passionately fond.

† This was a puff, I believe, of the labours of Sir H. Lawrence and Major MacGregor, who performed the Augean task of draining the filthiest capital in India.

‡ The Sikh officer's sympathy with his friend's love of the garden is especially pretty, because the Sikhs themselves, with totally contrary dispositions to the Afghans, care little for either trees or flowers. (R.

can I hope, therefore, that in the society of old friends, you will not also forget *me* ? But as in the daily intercourse of the last four months *I have seen the candour and openness* of your disposition, your *manly activity and disregard of toil*, your *fortitude and spirit in difficulties*, and above all your desire rather to earn for the young Maharajah among his Afghan subjects *as great a reputation for justice and lenity as his predecessors acquired for cruelty and violence*, so it was impossible I should not conceive an esteem for you, and a wish to continue our friendship.

" Remembering, therefore, how fond you are of the chase, and how often you have admired my English greyhounds, I now beg your acceptance of them ; that when the cold weather comes again, and with hawk and hound you once more take the field : when all your fat Punjābee dogs are panting in vain after the hare, and these swift runners catch her on the very edge of the forest, you will cry, ' *Shábásh !* ' (Well done !) and in a moment of pleasure remember me."

# CHAPTER III.

THUS, in the constancy of his justice and kindness, trusted; and in every civil and military method of action approved, Sir Herbert retires from the province for that time, with beautifully simple exposition of his farther purposes in the following proclamation :—

"Bunnoochees! I have laboured hard to do what I thought best for your own interests, for I love freedom as much as you; but you have rejected my interference, and proved yourselves incapable of gratitude for the forbearance which has been shown you by this Sikh army, which was able any day to rout all your tribes.

"Now mark my words. I have explored your valley, and know its riches; I have discovered your hidden road; I have counted your four hundred forts; I have estimated your tribes; and I will beg of my Government to let me come back to you again. I will lead in another army by the new way, and level your forts, and

disarm your tribes, and occupy your country.
You shall not be punished for your present
resistance.   No !   This beautiful scene shall no
more be desolated by revenge.   You shall have
the best laws that an enlightened people can
frame for you ; but they will be administered by
a Sikh Governor.   He cannot oppress you, for
the English will be over him.   You shall be justly
ruled, but you shall be free no more."

This extremely undiplomatic and serenely explicit
document being left for the wholesome food of the
Bunnoochee mind during the summer, Sir Herbert
returns with due punctuality on the 8th of December,
nominally " accompanying," practically in command
of, two very sufficient divisions of Sikh and Afghan
soldiery.   One of these divisions was formed at
Peshawur, consisting of three regiments of Sikh
infantry, one of regular cavalry, one troop of horse
artillery, and a thousand Afghan irregular horse.
It was conducted by Lieutenant George Reynell
Taylor.   To reach Bunnoo, it had to perform a very
difficult march over the Salt range.   The paths were
impassable by carts, and the Sikhs had to carry
their ammunition and stores on their heads.   The
guns were dismounted and carried on elephants,
which animals and camels are the only carriage an
army can use in this pass, (*pass*, in verity, the ravine

being at one place so narrow that it requires nice steering to prevent a camel's load being knocked off his back). The march, of roughly something over a hundred miles, sixty-four koss (a koss varying from one and a half to two miles), occupied seventeen days.

Meantime another proclamation, in Sir Herbert's coolly crystalline manner, is sent in advance, for the study of the still refractory provincials.

## " PROCLAMATION.

### " TO THE MULLICKS AND PEOPLE OF BUNNOO.

" I told you last spring, that if you did not accept the easy terms which I offered you, and pay up your arrears, I should come to collect the balance in the winter, build a fort, establish a Sikh garrison, and put your fertile valley under a Kárdár,* like any other part of the Punjāb kingdom.

" I am now on my way to keep my word ; and two forces are marching upon Bunnoo, one from Dera Ishmael Khan, and one from Peshawur.

---

* Kárdár means literally, in Persian, an agent ; but was commonly used in the Punjāb to designate a provincial collector of government revenue. In all cases, he had police functions ; in many, magisterial ; and in some even, judicial. He was thus armed with great power ; was generally supported by the Sikh Durbar, whether right or wrong, if he only bribed the courtiers well enough ; and was consequently a blessing or a curse, simply in the ratio of his own personal inclinations.

" You see, therefore, that you had much better have agreed with me in the spring.

" It still depends, however, on yourselves, how you will be treated.

" My orders are these : to collect your arrears of revenue, and make a settlement for the future.

" With respect to the first, you all know how much you owe, and the sooner you pay it, the better it will be for you. I have got all your accounts, and see that Lal Baz Khan's was the only tuppeh* which paid up. Lal Baz Khan shall have no reason to repent his good behaviour, for I shall give him a larger allowance than any other Mullick in Bunnoo.

" With respect to the future settlement, not only the claims of the Maharajah, but also of the Mullicks, of the Ryots, of the Syuds, and all other holy men who hold charitable lands, will be taken into consideration, and justice done to all.

" You know very well that no 'Sahib't ever fixes a heavy revenue. 'Sahibs' are at this moment settling the revenue throughout the Punjáb, and making all the people happy.

---

* Freehold farm.

† 'Sahib' means simply a master, and is distinctively and universally applied, throughout British India and the neighbouring countries, to Englishmen ; an involuntary confession of the master-energy of that race.

" If you wish for peace and kindness, therefore, and to be good subjects of the Maharajah, let the Mullicks present themselves in my camp without delay, and the people stay quietly in their houses.

" Last spring, half of you ran away to the hills ; some because they were afraid of being treated barbarously by the Sikhs, as usual, and some to escape paying revenue.

" You saw that I did not allow plundering, and that the soldiers were set as sentries over your crops, and therefore you need not now run away out of fear.

" And it is of no use your running away to avoid payment of revenue, because the Kárdár and garrison will wait till you come back, and you will at last either have to pay or remain for ever in exile.

" Let all good subjects therefore fear nothing, but pursue their labours of harvest and cultivation : and let every Mullick who does not wish to be ejected from his chieftainship come in to me.

" Above all keep in mind that the army which is now coming to Bunnoo, is not going away again after a month, but is coming to stay. Make your calculations therefore accordingly.

(Dated)

" Camp, Meeánee, November 17th, 1847."

These topics of meditation being presented to the

scholastic mind of the Bunnoochee dwellers in the
plain, Sir Herbert has next to consider what manner
of influence he may exercise on the mountaineers
above them and around, who are beyond the reach
of proclamation, and beyond the limits of rule—a
race whose life cannot be changed, nor liberties
touched. *Friendship* is possible with them, otherwise, the country may, perhaps, be swept clear of
them, and left desert ; subdued, they cannot be.

" The Vizeerees are at once one of the most
numerous and the most united of all the tribes of
Afghanistan ; and to this, not less than to the
strength of their country, are they indebted for
being wholly independent. They neither own now,
nor by their own account have ever owned, any
allegiance to any of the Kings of Cabul. If you
ask where their country is, they point to the far-off
horizon, where the azure sky is pierced by the
snowy peaks of ' Sufeyd Koh,' or the White
Mountain ; but that great mountain is only their
citadel, at the head of a long line of fastnesses
extending from the frontier of Tâk, less than
a hundred miles from Dera Ishmael Khan, on
the Indus, to within fifty miles from Jellalabad.
Hardy, and for the most part pastoral, they subsist
on mountains where other tribes would starve ; and
might enjoy the possession they have obtained of

most of the hills which encrust the valleys of Khost, Dour, and Bunnoo, without any inconvenience to the lawful owners in the plains below, if their pastoral cares were confined to their own cattle, and not extended to that of their neighbours. But it is the peculiarity of the great Vizeeree tribe that they are enemies of the whole world. Amongst themselves dissension is unknown, a spectacle unique in all Afghanistan ; and they are thus free to turn their whole strength outwards against weaker and more distracted races. Of the Vizeeree it is literally true, that 'his hand is against every man, and every man's hand against him.' By far the greater part of the trade between Khorassan and India comes and goes through the Pass of Gwaleyree, which emerges on the plain of the Indus, at the issue of the Gomul river, in Tâk. The hills on either side of the pass are held by the Otmanzye Vizeerees ; and they carry on a predatory war against the caravans, year after year, with a relentless ferocity and daring which none but a Lohânee (or an English) merchant would brave, or be able to repel.*

* " No quarter is given to men in these wars ; it is said that the Vizeerees would even kill a male child that fell into their hands ; but they never molest women, and if one of that sex wanders from her caravan, they treat her with kindness, and send guides to escort her to her tribe."—Elphinstone's ' Cabul,' vol. ii. p. 80.

This chivalric trait I can easily believe, though I never heard of it

Between the eastern cultivated lands of Bunnoo and the hills of the Khuttuks lies a wide, undulating waste, called the 'Thull,' or desert. It is not exactly a desert, because it furnishes vast herds with pasture every winter ; but it is a wilderness to any but the savage, taught by long experience to direct his path over it by the peaks of the surrounding mountains. Towards Bunnoo it is all sand, which nearer the hills gets hardened by a layer of gravel and loose stones washed down by the annual floods. Both the sand and the stony ground only require rain to make them yield abundant crops ; but rain seldom visits either, and the tract consequently is in general only dotted over with scrubby vegetation and the prickly bushes of the camel-thorn.

Even this is a paradise to the Vizeeree tribes, who, expelled from their own stony and pine-clad mountains by the snow, yearly set before them their flocks of broad-tailed sheep and goats, and strings of woolly camels and curved-eared horses, and migrate to the sheltered plains of Bunnoo. Here they stretch their blankets or reed mats on the bare

from other sources ; for considerable intercourse with the Vizeerees impressed me most favourably with their character, in spite of all the trouble their turbulent habits gave me. They are truly very noble savages.—H. B. E.

earth, over two sticks set up like the letter T, the four sides draggling on the ground, or fastened with a stone if the wind gets high. Under this miserable shelter huddle men, women, and children, afraid neither of the rain's cold nor the sun's hot beams, and in happy ignorance of better things. From the corner of the tent the shaggy muzzle of a hill sheep-dog peeps out and watches over the tethered donkey and sick goat left at home with the women while the flocks are out at graze. Tall and stately as a pine, the daughter of the mountains stands at the tent-door in her indigo-dyed petticoat and hood, smiling on the gambols of her naked brats, or else sits down and rubs out corn for her lord who is afield. The men, stout, fierce, and fearless of man or beast, and clad in shaggy cloaks of brown camel's-hair, drive out the herds to feed, and, with long juzail in hand, and burning match, lie full-length along the ground and listen for strange footfalls on the horizon. Should an enemy approach, the discharge of a single matchlock would be heard over the whole plain, and summon thousands of the tribe to the point where danger threatened or plunder allured. Such were the people whose gipsy-like encampments strewed the Thull at the time I speak of."

A people not studious of proclamations,—to be

dealt with, if at all, otherwise than by forms of law. What will Sir Herbert do with them ?

He leaves his army behind him in the plain, takes five-and-twenty horsemen with him, and rides into the midst of them.   His proclamation to the people of the plain is dated from the " Vizeeree Wells."

" From the Khuttuk hills, east of Kummur, a deep and broad ravine runs down into the Thull.   In seasons of flood it is the bed of an impetuous torrent called the Lowâghur, but during the greater part of the year is dry, the little water which soaks down from the hills being insufficient to rise to the surface. To reach this water at all seasons (without which their flocks would perish), the Vizeerees have descended into the ravine (which at Joor was from forty to fifty feet deep at least), and there scraped wells about the depth of a man's stature.   Round the margin of the wells clay troughs were formed, into which a Vizeeree, standing in the well, ladled up water for the thirsty cattle.   Inclined planes were also scraped in the high banks of the ravine for the cattle to go up and down ; and the sand in every direction, both round the wells on the slopes and on the plains around, was deeply imprinted with the hoofs of myriads of sheep and oxen who were daily driven here to water.

In these our days it is rarely the fortune of

civilized man to stand in such a spot to behold a
genuine primæval, pastoral people, and in thought
see Time visibly put back to the days of Lot and
Abraham, who had flocks and herds and tents.

Not a house, or hut, or field, was to be seen
in this wild spot ; and, save for an occasional thin
column of smoke, seen for a moment in the sandy
distance, and then lost in the blue sky, we might
have deemed ourselves out of the reach of man.
But, in truth, we were in the very heart of ' The
Vizeerees,' a name of terror even to the barbarous
tribes of Bunnoo.

How dared we, then, with our small party,
venture there ?  For the present, the reader must
be content to know that it was purely on the faith
of a friendship which I had formed in the former
expedition with Swahn Khan, the most powerful
man of his powerful nation.  An inhabitant of the
snowy mountains, he had never descended to do
homage to Sikh invaders, and Cabul kings had
never ventured among his hills.  Yet he had asked
to be allowed to come down and speak with the
fellow-countryman of Moorcroft, the traveller, from
whom he showed me a scrap of paper, dated
' Dummáee Thull, April 6th, 1824.'  It merely
acknowledged Swahn Khan's hospitality and civility ;
and after keeping it for twenty-three years, the far-

sighted Vizeeree chief had lived to see the day
when the white man's armies should tread upon the
heels of the white man's pioneer.  It was time to
draw forth from his goat-skin wallet the record of
his good faith towards an Englishman, certain that
that faded 'certificate' of the solitary, helpless
traveller, would now be as strong to him as an
army !

I could not but regard the MS. with warm but
melancholy interest.  He who wrote it had long
since ended his earthly wanderings.  That adven-
turous spirit had breathed its last among the
savages of Andkhoo, beyond the remotest confines
of Afghanistan.

This scratch of his pen survived, and was only
just beginning to fulfil the grateful purpose with
which it was given to the Vizeeree host.  It
reminded me of the aloe, which is so long before
it flowers ; or of those sealed bottles, which have
sometimes been found in tombs, and when opened
give up the perfume of a forgotten age.

I am glad to be able to contribute the smallest
white pebble to poor Moorcroft's cairn ; and cannot
pass on without recording that my friend Swahn
Khan spoke of him highly in every way, adding
that 'he was very wise, and wrote down everything :
the trees, the crops, the stones, the men and women,

their clothes and household furniture, and everything! He also gave medicine to their sheep and
horses, and' (climax of ability in a Vizeeree
country) 'cured them all!'

Fully as much in honour of Moorcroft's memory,
as with any view to future profit, I made Swahn
Khan my guest ; sent a 'Ziyâfut,' or welcoming
present, of one hundred rupees to his tent, and
ordered five rupees a day to be given to himself,
and two pounds of flour to each of his followers
as long as they chose to stay with me. The rude
chief, who possessed all the virtues, with few of the
vices, of a savage people, never forgot this treatment ; and scarcely had I reached Michenkheyl, on
the 2nd December, in this second expedition, than
I found myself locked in his giant arms, and
squeezed till I could have cried. It was he who
had now guided our force to 'The Wells' in the
desert, and whose presence in our camp made us
as secure in the winter pasture grounds of the
Vizeerees, as though we had been in the citadel of
Lahore.

To the best of my belief, therefore, I was the
first European who had ever been seen in the
Vizeeree Thull ; yet my full confidence in the
honour of Swahn Khan, who undertook to guide me,
may be gathered from the circumstance that I took

with me only five-and-twenty horsemen, and those
at his request, in case of any casual opposition from
tribes over whom the Vizeeree had no control. I
pause upon this apparently trifling incident, for no
foolish vanity of my own, but for the benefit of
others ; for hoping, as I earnestly do, that many a
young soldier glancing over these pages will gather
heart and encouragement for the stormy lot before
him, I desire above all things to put into his hand
the staff of confidence in his fellow-man.

> ' Candid, and generous, and just,
>      Boys care but little whom they trust—
>           An error soon corrected :
>      For who but learns in riper years,
>      That man, when smoothest he appears,
>           Is most to be suspected ? '

is a verse very pointed and clever, but quite un-
worthy of ' The Ode to Friendship,' and inculcating
a creed which would make a sharper or a monk of
whoever should adopt it. The man who cannot
trust others is, by his own showing, untrust-
worthy himself. Suspicious of all, depending on
himself for everything, from the conception to the
deed, the ground-plan to the chimney-pot, he will
fail for want of the heads of Hydra and the hands
of Briareus. If there is any lesson that I have
learnt from life, it is that human nature, black or

white, is better than we think it ; and he who reads
these pages to a close will see how much faith I
have had occasion to place in the rudest and
wildest of their species, how nobly it was deserved,
and how useless I should have been without it."

From the Vizeeree wells, then, Sir Herbert dates
his second proclamation, to the "landlords and
priests" of Bunnoo, in the following decisive terms.

## "PROCLAMATION.

### "TO THE MULLICKS AND SYUDS OF BUNNOO.

"The force from Peshawur has this morning
joined General Cortlandt's, and to-morrow I shall
enter Bunnoo with eighteen guns, one hundred and
thirty zumbooruhs, two thousand cavalry, and five
regiments of infantry.

"Almost all the Mullicks of Bunnoo have wisely
come in ; but two or three are still absent, and I
now warn them for the last time, that unless they
come in they will be dealt with as enemies.

"The people of Bunnoo, it is well known, are
entirely in the hands of their religious advisers (the
Syuds, etc.), and their Mullicks.   I now give notice,
therefore, that in whatsoever tuppeh a single shot is
fired upon the Sikh camp, or a Sikh soldier, in that
tuppeh I will depose the Mullick from all authority,
and confiscate his lands, and will not give one

beeguh * of ground in Dhurum-Urth † to any holy man.

"On this you may rely. And it will not be admitted as any excuse that bad characters from one tuppeh came into another and there fired upon my men. I hold the masters and priests responsible for the peace of their own tuppeh.

(Dated)

" 8th December, Camp, Vizeeree Wells."

" Next morning we marched from ' The Wells ' to Jhundookheyl, about ten miles, and encamped in Bunnoo Proper, on the left bank of the Khoorrum, without any opposition, and the same evening Bazeed Khan, Zubburdust Khan, and Khilát Khan, three Sooraunee tuppeh chiefs, and Meer Alum Khan, of Mundaie, all great malcontents who had hitherto stood aloof, and the latter one of the most dangerous men in Bunnoo, came sulkily in and made their submission.

The only Bunnoochee chief who had not now

---

* A beeguh is a land measure of which I have forgotten the precise extent in the countries Trans-Indus. Professor Duncan Forbes, in his invaluable dictionary (Hindustaní and English), says it is, in Bengal, about one-third of an English acre, and in the upper provinces about five-eighths.

† Dhurum-Urth means a "religious object," and means, in the Punjáb, a charitable grant of any kind.

4

surrendered was the celebrated Dilassuh Khan, who deserves a more particular notice. By right he was only lord of one-quarter of one of the tuppehs, Dâood Shâh ; but his desperate and cruel character had secured the whole. He was distinguished above all his countrymen for implacable enmity, and the bravest hostility to the Sikhs : on one occasion Dewan Tara Chund, at the head of eight thousand Sikhs and twelve guns, was repulsed from his fort with a loss of two hundred killed and five hundred wounded ; and on another occasion when attacked by Rajah Soocheyt Singh, one of the bravest chiefs in the Sikh army, with ten thousand men, Dilassuh stood a siege of two days in a weak mud fort, and then forced his way out at night. (I believe it was on the former of these two occasions that the guns had all the advantage of being directed by a French officer, General Court !)

In short, Dilassuh Khan had passed his life in waging war with the Sikh invaders, who never entered Bunnoo without thinking of him with dread, and never left it without fresh cause to remember and hate him. When I accompanied the first expedition to Bunnoo, as much to my surprise as that of all the Sikh soldiers, Dilassuh, for the first time in his life, came in, saying without circumlocution, though in the presence of many Sikh

chiefs, that 'he could trust a Sahib! but if I had
not been with the force, neither he would be sitting
there quietly nor the Sikh army!' He was then a
grey-headed old rebel of seventy, but his determined
features, knit brows and flashing eye, showed that
he had lost none of the fire of youth; he came in
rather proudly, with fifty or sixty horsemen at his
back, but I was glad of it, as it attracted all the
old Sikhs in camp to look at him through the
screens of my tent as if he had been a caged tiger.
Till then I had no idea of his importance, but
gathered it very soon from the muttered impre-
cations and expressions of surprise which broke
from the veterans whom he had so often harassed.
On the whole, however, they did him justice, and
said, 'He is a great man; other chiefs have more
followers, but Dilassuh has honour!'

Dilassuh upon this occasion remained an honoured
guest in my camp for about a month, when our line
of march bringing us near his fort, Sirdar Shumsher
Singh, the Sikh chief with whom I was associated,
could not forbear from riding out to see the stronghold which had cost his countrymen so much blood;
and the Sikh troopers who formed his escort took
the opportunity of riding round and about it in
an insulting manner which they would have most
carefully eschewed had the old Bunnoochee rebel

been in arms. The consequence was, that Dilassuh considered this as a reconnoissance preparatory to a bombardment, and fled that very night to the Dour hills, whence I was never again able to recal him. He thought, as most Asiatics would, that I was privy to the Sirdar's design, and that I had all along been cajoling him with apparent kindness only the the more surely to destroy him and avenge my Sikh allies. In short, I had lost his confidence, and in the bitterness of his awakened passions he wrote me a most insulting letter from his mountain lair, which had I caught him again at that time I most certainly would have made him swallow before I took him back into favour ; but it was better as it was. On my return now to Bunnoo I felt compassion for the difficulty the old chief was in, and sincerely respecting his career of patriotism, was unwilling to drive so brave and aged a man into exile for the few years he had still to live. I wrote therefore on the 9th of December to tell him that if he did not come in for fear of being punished for his late misconduct he might reassure himself, and accept my guarantee for his life and honour ; but if he meant to go into open rebellion I should have no alternative but to make an example of him. On receipt of this he was inclined to come in and 'trust to his destiny' ; but he had many enemies, who were jealous of his great name, and the honour I had shown him when he was my guest, and they treacherously advised him 'to fly and die as he had lived, a rebel.' Dilassuh took their advice, fled to Dour, and never while I was there returned to Bunnoo, though he tried in vain to come at the head of an invading army. I think it due to Major Reynell Taylor to add, that when he succeeded me in Bunnoo, Dilassuh asked and readily received permission to return to his native country. A severer punishment could not be inflicted on him than to let him see the revolution which a few months had effected in the once strong and formidable valley : the boasted forts all level with the earth, a fortress of the Crown alone looking down upon the now open and peaceful villages ; the peasantry unarmed ; a broad road traversing the country ; peace reigning where there was once perpetual feud ; a government where all was anarchy ; the Sikhs lords, and Dilassuh nothing !

To resume the thread of our narrative, Dilassuh was the only Bunnoochee chief who had not come in on the 9th of December."

"Come in,"—-that is to say, presented himself at the English head-quarters under truce, and as ready to enter into pacific negotiation. Nothing yet concluded, and every chief able to retire into his fort at his pleasure, and stand at bay behind his battle-ments. The matter is to be considered of ; but the Vizeerees must be finally dealt with first.

" The reader will not have forgotten that on December 11th, Swahn Khan, Vizceree, had agreed to lay my terms before the rest of his countrymen ; and promised that the jeerga, or council, should give their final decision in a week. Many of the grey-beards of the tribes were absent at the time in the hills, and had to be summoned ; and when they arrived, there was such difference of opinion as to the propriety of submission or resistance that, for the first time in the history of the Vizeerees, there seemed likely to be an internal feud.

Thus matters stood at the sixth day (Dec. 16th), when all the leading chiefs adjourned the jeerga to my camp. There, under a large awning, outside my tent-door, these wild savages seated themselves in a circle on a carpet, and awaited with proud dignity my entry with the written proposals. In idler days I would have given anything for such a group to sketch, as, clothed in their storm-stained mantles of camel's hair, with long elfin locks of rusty black or grey, dyed red with henna, hanging about their shoulders and weather-beaten counten-ances, each grasped his brass-bound juzail, or felt that his knife was loose within his girdle, in case

the Feringhee chief should have drawn them into an
ambush under pretence of a council.   But now I had
no leisure for such light amusement ; and it was
with a deep sense of the importance of our mutual
object, and the peace or war depending on the issue,
that I seated myself among them, and read, in
Persian, the following paper.

The Vizeerees bent their heads to listen with as
much attention as if they had been scholars : and
then, at the close of each paragraph, turned eagerly
to a chief from a neighbouring Afghan valley, whose
education and friendship with the Vizeerees had
made me select him as interpreter.

'TERMS OFFERED TO THE CHIEFS OF THE
VIZEEREE TRIBES, IN JEERGA ASSEMBLED.

' I find  that in the course of the twenty-five or
thirty years which have elapsed  since the country
of Bunnoo was separated from the Khorassánee
empire, the Vizeerees have taken advantage of their
own unanimity and the divisions of the Bunnoochees
to invade this fertile valley, and possess themselves
little by little of extensive tracts of land.

' You did this at a time when there was no ruler,
and no law in Bunnoo ; and if among themselves the
Bunnoochees respected no man's rights, but acted
on the principle that land belonged to whoever was

strong enough to seize it, they cannot complain if you followed their example. Foreigners are always expected to adopt the customs of the country.

'That time has, however, gone. The Lahore Sirkar* has determined to occupy Bunnoo, and for the future there will be a fort and an army, a hâkim and laws, the same as in any other part of the Punjāb kingdom.

'The object of this is to secure the payment of the revenue ; and a survey is now being made of every tuppeh to ascertain how much land there is, and who holds it.

'Whoever holds land in Bunnoo, whether he be a Bunnoochee, a Khuttuk, a Vizeeree, or of any other country, will have to pay revenue alike. No favour will be shown to any tribe, great or small, strong or weak ; all landholders in Bunnoo will be considered as Bunnoochees.

'Mullick Swahn Khan tells me that the Vizeerees have never paid revenue to any king, and they do not see why they should now.

'This argument is very good as long as you stay in your own country, which is still independent. Maharajah Duleep Singh has nothing to say to the

---

* 'Sirkar,' the sovereign or supreme authority in the state. In a private household the idiom is often aped out of affectation, or used by a servant out of flattery.

Vizeeree hills ; but when you come down into his country of Bunnoo you must submit to his laws.

‘ If you do not like laws, and paying revenue, you are quite at liberty to give up your lands to the Bunnoochees, from whom you took them, and return to those happy hills where there is no revenue to give and no corn to eat.

‘ Of one thing be assured, that I will either make you pay revenue like the Bunnoochees, or expel you from Bunnoo.   I have troops enough here to destroy your whole tribe.

‘ I do not believe, however, that you will be fools enough to forsake in a day the lands which you have been thirty years in conquering, or forego the whole of your rich harvests rather than pay a part.

‘ I therefore offer you the following terms :—

‘ First. All lands purchased in the tuppehs of Bunnoo, or that have been violently retained in the possession of Vizeerees for five years, shall be confirmed to the holders, as well as any of more recent date, if possession has not been opposed.

‘ Secondly. On these lands you shall pay revenue at the same rate as the Bunnoochees.

‘ Thirdly.  The extensive grazing ground, called the Thull, which is bounded by the Khuttuk lands on the east ; Durreh-i-Tung, on the south ; Michun-

kheyl, on the west ; and the mouth of the
Khoorrum, on the north,—shall be given up to
you for your flocks and herds, on condition of
allegiance ; and that each year when your tribes
come down from the hills, your Mullicks come in
to the Kárdár of Bunnoo, report the number of
the tribes which have come down, and present a
yearly nuzzurana of two hundred and fifty fat
doombuhs ; the shares paid by each tribe to be
settled among yourselves.

' Fourthly. On any land cultivated in the Thull,
either by yourselves or others, you shall pay one-
sixth of the produce.*

' Fifthly. As your tribes are scattered about over
so large a surface, Mullick Swahn Khan shall be
appointed to conduct all business between the Sirkar
and the Vizeerees ; and shall be called the Vizeer
of the Vizeerees of Bunnoo, and Mullick of the
Thull.

---

* The cultivation I had seen in the Thull, had almost all been the
work of Khuttuks, of a subdivision called Sooltan Kheyl, who are
subjects properly of Esaukheyl. The speculators paid, I was told, one-
sixth to the Vizeerees for the privilege of cultivating ground which the
Vizeerees annually appropriated to the pasture of flocks. I therefore
now purposely fixed the land revenue of the Thull so low as one-sixth,
to allow of the above arrangement continuing ; for if one-sixth comes
to us, and one-sixth to the Vizeerees, two-thirds will still be left
with the farmers ; and that is a remunerating share, all the world
over.

'Sixthly. All emnity shall cease between the Vizeerees and the Bunnoochees; and there shall be no quarrelling, and murdering, and plundering, and drying up of each others' canals. Any Vizeeree who thinks himself aggrieved will get speedy justice from me.

'Think over these things deliberately, and then give me a decisive answer, Yes or No.

(Dated)
'16th December, 1847.'

At the close of each paragraph the Vizeerees watched my countenance to see if I was satisfied with my friend's interpretation in Pushtoo, a language of which I knew about as much as they did of Persian. The little I did know was however quite sufficient to enable me, knowing the subject, to follow the explanation of an interpreter, and tell whether he kept back any essential point. Necessity and habit soon make a man, thrown on his own resources as I was, expert in exercising this indispensable check on interpretation; and wild races, especially, who have not yet learnt the hypocrisy of courts, but use their muscles as God intended, knitting their brows when they are angry, and laughing loud when they are pleased, exhibit involuntarily on their faces a register of the meaning which the ear has reported to the brain.

As soon as the Vizeerees were satisfied that they had been made masters of my real meaning, they next proceeded to discuss its bearing on their interests ; and the debate soon got so warm, that for decency's sake they adjourned it to their own camp, where they could speak as loud as they liked. My spies went with them, and had the pleasure of hearing all the arguments over again on the road, and then a third time in the Vizeeree camp. Words here ran very high, and my friend Mullick Swahn Khan was roundly accused of selling himself and his tribe to me ; but as all were of opinion that the Bunnoochees would never co-operate honestly in any plan of hostilities, so no one ventured to recommend resistance ; and the jeerga sternly returned at last to make an un-conditional surrender. I caused each chief to sign the ' terms,' or rather, to make a scratch where he was told ; and as none of them had ever had a pen in their hands before,* much laughter was occasioned by this first approach to the slavery of civilization ; and the assembly broke up in good humour, to which I further contributed by a feast in honour of the new alliance.

It is difficult for the English reader of these

* How Sir Herbert's conscience could ever rest, after he had put one into them, I understand not.—J. R.

pages, or indeed any one unacquainted with Bunnoo and the tribes around, to estimate the importance of this consummation; but there was no one in camp, from General Cortlandt, who commanded, down to the lânguree cooking the Sikh soldiers' dinner, who did not feel that the most difficult half of our task in that country was now accomplished.

In round numbers, the Vizeerees were said to be in possession of one-third of the valley; their stout mud forts studded the whole length of the eastern tuppehs; and their tribes, driven down by the cold, were at that season swarming in the adjacent Thull. Warlike and predatory from the natural necessities of a barren country, bold from never having been subdued, possessing the rare quality among Afghans of unanimity, and so savage in their wars that even the Bunnoochees thought themselves lambs in comparison, it is impossible to deny that the Vizeerees would have been most harassing enemies at that present time; and though ultimately we should have doubtless found an opportunity of inflicting severe chastisement upon them, the war would have been resumed the next year, and a continual system of forays and reprisals have kept Bunnoo in a ferment. As it was, the submission of the Vizeerees extinguished the brightest spark of hope in the Bunnoochees. They were now left to their own resources, and the only chance of a successful insurrection was in the levelling of their forts. Those strongholds of rebellion had yet to be thrown down. The foundations of our own were not yet dug."

# CHAPTER IV.

" IN the Introductory Chapter, it will be remembered that the two main points of the military plan I laid before Government, for the reduction of Bunnoo, were *to raze to the ground all the forts of the Bunnoochees, and build one large one for the Crown.* The question was, how to do either one or the other in a hostile country, with an armed population ; and which to attempt first ? A lawless state of society had obliged men to herd together for mutual protection ; and whether a dozen houses or a hundred were thus united, the whole invariably took the form of a fort, and were cemented into one 'walled city,' equally impregnable by the ruffian horsemen of their own country or the well-appointed cavalry of the Sikhs. Nor was the direct fire of artillery of much more avail, for the mud made out of the soil of Bunnoo is of such extraordinary tenacity when hardened by the sun, that to breach the wall of a fort was next to impossible. In the lower part, where it was thick, no impression was made ; the ball lodged, and there was an end of it; nothing was brought down.   In the upper part, at the height of twenty or thirty feet from the ground, where the mud wall tapered to the thinness of a man's arm, a cannon shot went through, and left a round hole exactly its own size ; and this operation might have been continued till the upper part of the whole wall was like a nutmeg grater or sieve ; yet the whole thing would stand as firmly as a plate of perforated zinc let into a building for ventilation.   The only rapid ways of taking such forts, were first by throwing in shells, and burning the garrison out, by firing the village inside ; secondly, by powder bags, as Major Thompson took Ghuznee ;  or,  thirdly,  by running a gun up to the gate, and blowing it in ; and the first was probably the least hazardous. Supposing, then, the most favourable circumstances : that our force was able to take, and raze, one fort daily,  and  that  our  doing  so  did  not  irritate  the population to rise *en masse*, and bring on general hostilities ;  then  it  was  clear  that  it  would  take upwards of a year to level all the forts, about four hundred in number ; and the soldiers of the force would be exposed, day after day, to the inclemency of the sun at one season, and the rains at another. In my judgment, that was an operation which no troops  could  carry  through,  and  ought  not  to  be asked to attempt; and I willingly embraced the only alternative of making the people level their own forts with their own hands. This, however, was an experiment to be very cautiously approached; and I determined, first of all, to commence a fort for ourselves, and complete it to the height of an intrenched position, so as to be able to leave half of my force in safety within it, while I moved out with the other half against any Bunnoochee Mullick who refused to raze his fort.

Having settled this in my own mind, the next thing was to choose a site for our fort. This was a most difficult thing to do in a new, and enemy's country; yet, on doing it judiciously depended not merely the security and comfort of the garrison, but also its efficiency as a controlling force.

It was impossible to be many days in Bunnoo, even on the first expedition, without having misgivings as to the possibility of ever making a settlement with the Bunnoochees, which should have for its basis the voluntary payment of an annual revenue; and anticipating the ultimate necessity of a military occupation, I early made inquiries after a good position for the erection of a royal fort. By a good position, I mean an influential one: for a strong natural position was not to be expected in that level and highly cultivated valley. Perhaps the strongest

5

in Bunnoo is Akra, the site of an old Greek city
(which I shall describe elsewhere) ; but, unfortu-
nately for my purpose, this was close to the border
of Murwut, the least dignified position which a force
of occupation could take up ; for we should have had
very much the air of being prepared to run away at
a moment's notice.    After much anxious deliberation,
I finally selected a spot called Bureyree, within a
stone's throw of the great canal of Kooch Kote, and
I think about a mile from the town of Bazaar.    It
was (rather treacherously) pointed out to General
Cortlandt by Mullick Jaffir, Khan of Ghoreewâl ;
and Lal Baz Khan, the chief of that town, afterwards told me that ' he had watched us wheeling
round and round like a hawk, and could not think
what game we were hunting till he saw us come
pounce down upon Bureyree.    Then he knew it was
for a fort.    Many a Bunnoochee Mullick had longed
to build there, but the others all joined to prevent
him, for fear he should be master of Kooch
Kote.'

*December* 18*th*, 1847.—To-day, at noon, the
foundation of our fort was actually commenced
on the chosen site at Bureyree.    To please the
Sikhs, the usual native ceremonies were performed :
the soil turned up, and oil poured in ; sweetmeats
distributed, a royal salute of twenty-one guns

fired, and the infant fort named 'Duleepgurh,' in honour of the little Maharajah whose sovereignty it is intended to establish. To-morrow we march to the spot and encamp there, so as to protect and superintend the workmen.

I do not think that, up to this time, the Bunnoochees believed that it was really intended to occupy their country. The idea seemed to them too absurd. The natural obstacles of the valley; the savage hatred of the Mahometan people ; and the innumerable forts in which they took refuge when worsted, and whence they seldom or never could be expelled, had sufficed, for a quarter of a century, to disgust the Sikhs with the very name of Bunnoo ; and the Bunnoochees, in consequence, had got into the habit of believing that no foreign invader could put them to greater inconvenience than a temporary sojourn in the adjoining hills. So long, therefore, as our army was not indulged in its ancient licence, but was kept in strict discipline, they had little or no objection to its marching and counter-marching about the valley ; and they devoutly believed, that when the cold season ended, the fiery sun, whose rays are collected into an intolerable focus between the surrounding hills, would as quickly drive us away again to the Punjāb as it had done on the last occasion. It seemed, then, to them, the wisest policy not to oppose us openly by arms; but, on the contrary, to yield apparently to all demands; and to this, quite as much as to their own quarrels, we were indebted for our unopposed advance. They permitted their lands to be measured, in the conviction that it was all a pretence to frighten them; and they slowly paid in very harmless instalments of their arrears, for fear we should see that our flimsy artifice had been penetrated. The settlement with the Vizeerees gave the first shock to this blissful delusion, for it had every appearance of being real; but there were not wanting those who maintained that even this hot contest had been cleverly got up between me and my friend Swahn Khan, the Vizeeree chief. The time, however, was now approaching when the Bunnoochees were to awake for ever from their dream of security. The digging of the foundation for a royal fort, the Hindū ceremonial of propitiating the earth,* the loud salute, and the dedication to the Maharajah, all bore marks of a work that was begun in earnest; and though the Solomons of the valley still winked at their duller neighbours, and maintained the joke to be as good as ever, the majority of the Bunnoochee peasantry, who looked on at the ceremony of the

---

* Not in the least shocking to Sir Herbert, you observe,—nor absurd nor objectionable in any wise—this Hindū ceremonial.

18th December, walked away with lengthened faces and saddened hearts. . . .

*December* 21*st.*—The different sides of the new fort were this day portioned out to the regiments to superintend and work at. Want tools; but think we shall run up the walls in six weeks.

The instructions I received from Colonel Lawrence as to this fort were as follow: * 'Build a good mud fort, capable of holding twelve hundred men and eight guns, in a healthy, centrical † position ; if possible, commanding the irrigation of the valley. Unless commanding a wholesome running stream, it should be furnished with wells or cisterns capable of holding water for the garrison for six months. Six of your guns can be put into the fort. Its peace garrison should be two companies of regular infantry, two hundred irregulars, and a company of artillery. In the next two or three years, four regiments of infantry, one of cavalry, five hundred or one thousand irregular horse, twelve guns, and fifty zumbooruhs, will remain in *one* cantonment near the fort : and on any disturbance arising, the mass of this force should at once proceed and put

* See 'The Punjâb Blue Book of 1847-9.' pp. 83, 84, where the instructions are given in full.

† ('Centrical,' having the faculty of radiating command in it,—though not absolutely 'central.')

it down, leaving their weakly men in the fort. The means of moving two regiments, six guns, and one thousand horse at an hour's notice, should be always kept up. Let your cantonment be as compact as possible, one face at least covered by the fort, and the further extremities covered by high mud towers, capable of each holding fifty men, and water and provisions for them for a week. All magazines and store-rooms to be in the fort, where six months' supplies for five hundred men should always be stored.'

It may easily be conceived how much I now felt the want of a military education, and that practical knowledge of field fortification which every cadet acquires (if he has got any sense, and wishes to be a soldier, and not a clothes-horse for red jackets) at either Addiscombe or Sandhurst. I had not had these advantages, and the consequence was that, though holding the commission of Lieutenant in an army belonging to the most civilized nation of the nineteenth century, I was driven to imitate the system of fortification which one of the most barbarous races of Asia may have inherited, for aught I know, from the dispersed architects of Babel. However, General Cortlandt* and I put

* In command of the Sikhs, under Lieutenant Edwardes, and Civil Governor of the Upper Trans-Indus.

our heads together, and made the best we could of the matter. Sitting up in my tent one bitter cold night, with scale and compass, pen and paper, we planned and elevated, and built up and knocked down, and dug imaginary ditches, and threw out flanking bastions, till, in our own opinion, we made the place very little inferior to Gibraltar.

The inner fort or citadel was to be one hundred yards square, its walls twenty feet high (including rampart of six feet), and nine feet thick. It was to be surrounded with a deep, dry ditch. The outer fort, or cantonment, eighty yards from the inner one, its walls ten feet high and six feet thick, and the whole surrounded with another ditch about thirty feet deep. Both ditches could be filled with water from a canal close by. The citadel was to contain lines for one native regiment, a magazine, and a commandant's house, which I intended to occupy if I stayed that year in Bunnoo. In the middle was to be a well. Four heavy guns were to mount the four inner bastions. The cantonment, or outer fort, was to contain lines for three more regiments of native infantry, one thousand cavalry, two troops of horse artillery, and eighty zumboo-ruhs, or camel-swivels. The two troops of horse artillery would be distributed in the four outer bastions, three guns in each. One side of the

outer fort was to be given up to the cavalry and
artillery horses, and camels of the zumbooruhs.

The plan of putting the cantonment round the
foot of the citadel as an outer wall was thought,
by both General Cortlandt and myself, better than
a separate inclosure at a distance; as, by our
arrangement, the fort and cantonment became a
mutual protection. As matters turned out, some
months afterwards, it might have saved the life of
the Commandant of the fort, had Colonel Lawrence's plan of separating the cantonment been
abided by; but, in building a fort, even Vauban
would not think it necessary to provide for such a
contingency as the citadel being besieged by its
own garrison! This, as the reader will see, was,
ere long, the fate of Duleepgurh.

Having thus projected our fort, we had next to
consider how to build it. It was not likely that we
should get many of the Bunnoochees to rivet their
own chains; and if we sent to the other side of
the Indus for workmen, great delay would be
occasioned. General Cortlandt informed me that
Runjeet Singh was in the habit of making the
Sikh army build their own forts, and quoted the
instances of Jumrood, Peshawur, Doond-Sahuttee,
Mozuffurabad, and Huzaruh; but there was nothing
they would not have done for their "great Maha-

rajah." Goolab Sing, and other powerful Sirdars, had also persuaded the armies they commanded to labour at fortifications ; but they did it by making an *amusement* of it, not a *duty*, and by themselves carrying a few blocks of stone, as an example. The present seemed to me an occasion when, whether it were an amusement or not, it was the imperative duty of the Sikh force to build the fort, which was to secure the interests of their sovereign, and their own personal safety ; and accordingly, on the 21st of December, as entered above in the Diary, 'the different sides of the fort were this day portioned out to the regiments,' etc. How this fared, the reader will soon see.

While these military plans were in operation, General Cortlandt, as Nazim or Civil Governor of the Upper Trans-Indus countries, was actively carrying on an under-current of civil duties ; and the stream, after passing him, ultimately came to me, as the court of confirmation and appeal. The business this involved was immense, for the late Governor, Dowlut Raie, had, in some way or other, reduced every province and every landholder to the lowest ebb. Now, all came to General Cortlandt for justice. The General, ever patient and pains-taking, bore up as well as he could against the mass of complaints which began to pour into

Bunnoo, from Esaukheyl, Murwut, Kolachee, and Dera Ishmael Khan ; but when he came over to my tent at sunset, he had usually as little appetite as I for dinner. My invaluable *chef*, Gholam Hoossain, would have created a feast in the midst of a desert, at half an hour's notice ; but his best chicken, stuck with pistachio-nuts, looked too like the ghost of one of Dowlut Raie's victims ; and the *soufflet*, on which he prided himself most, seemed to our weary vision the very embodiment of a monstrous injury. Dinner over, work was resumed by candlelight, and midnight generally passed before we got to bed.

The assistants of Colonel Lawrence in the Punjab at no time had ever to complain of too little to do, the work, during 1846, 7, and 8, varying from ten to fourteen hours per diem ; but I look back to these months in Bunnoo as the hardest grind I ever endured. Even the chiefs and peasantry of Bunnoo itself, though they might any day have been plunged into hostilities against us, began to appreciate the blessing of an impartial and honest tribunal, and, from looking on idly at the trials of Esaukheylees or Murwutees, soon changed into litigants on their own account, and promised, in a short while, to put every acre of the valley into Chancery. Seeing their minds thus prepared to welcome any system of regular laws, after the anarchy to which they had been used, I thought the time was come for imposing on them a simple code, adapted to their circumstances and understandings; the restrictions of which should interfere as little as possible with the free habits of individuals, while on their face they should be evidently for the general weal. Accordingly, the following entry appears in the Diary of the 21st of December.

*Last night, sat up and prepared a Proclamation of Law and Justice for Bunnoo, which I translated this morning into Persian.** Am doubtful whether the laws about arms will be sanctioned, but think them necessary; and if carefully acted up to, they will, in process of time, disarm the valley without violence.

## 'PROCLAMATION.

### 'CONCERNING THE ADMINISTRATION OF JUSTICE, AND LAWS TO BE OBSERVED IN BUNNOO.'

' 1. Henceforward all rule and justice rests with the Nazim of the province, who represents the Crown; and, in his absence, with the local Kárdár of the valley.

' 2. Mullicks have no authority, except to carry

---

* Italics mine. See what one man can do, with a good head and a warm heart !—J. R.

out the Nazim's or Kárdár's orders, and to collect the revenue of their respective tuppehs.

' 3. Any Bunnoochee or Vizeeree, therefore, who has a suit or complaint to prefer, must go to the Nazim or Kárdár, and give in a written representation of his case.

' 4. Law and justice being attainable by all, recourse to arms for the settlement of disputes is henceforth forbidden. Any person violating this rule is liable to be punished as a murderer, and if not hanged, will certainly be imprisoned for a term of years, perhaps for life. Let no one think that he will only be fined for cutting and wounding others. Fines will never be received in compensation of blood.*

' 5. When any murder or robbery is committed in or near a village, the Mullick and people of that village will be held responsible either to produce the murderers or robbers, or to carry the track on to

---

* This law 4 referred to the laws which were formerly in force under Runject Singh, in the Punjáb, by which there was a scale of offences against life and person, from murder downwards to assault, and a corresponding scale of fines, which, when levied, were shamelessly put into the royal treasury, instead of being given to the injured parties or their families, as they would have been had they made any pretence to justice. The price of a neighbour's life in this code was, if I remember rightly, eleven hundred rupees, or £110, so that the State made a good thing of a murder, and had great reason to complain of a simple case of maiming.

other villages, who in like manner must carry it out of their own boundary;* and the Mullick of every village will be fined if he does not give immediate information of such an event to the Mullick of the tuppeh, who will inform the Kárdár under a similar penalty. It is impossible for a murderer or a robber to bring home horses, sheep, cows, money or other plunder, without its being known in his own village ; and villages will accordingly be held responsible in twice the amount of the property stolen if they do not give information against the offenders.

' 6. These rules, the probability of discovery, and the certainty of punishment, being sufficient security for the lives of individuals, no man, whether Bunnoo-chee, Vizeeree, or other person in Bunnoo, except the military or police servants of the Government, will be allowed to carry musket, sword, spear, pistol, dagger, or other kind of arms. Any person violating this rule will be considered to do so with evil intent, and will be imprisoned, fined, or otherwise severely punished.

* This system of tracking, and village responsibility, was in general use in the Punjáb. and is almost the only way of detecting crime in countries where the people are not sufficiently civilized to be enlisted on the side of law, and against crime. Its justice is also obvious in communities which are for the most part brotherhoods or clans. The expertness of the Indian trackers is well known. and their untiring perseverance seldom fails to be rewarded with the apprehension of the hunted criminal.

' 7. The above rule applies also to strangers, and particularly to those tribes who on every Friday come in great numbers to buy and sell in the town of Bazaar.* Any stranger who conducts himself peaceably will receive the same protection from the Nazim or Kárdár, as if he was a subject of the Maharajah, but if he carries arms he will be imprisoned.

' 8. Any person who thinks the Government is unable to protect his village from attack, is at liberty to keep arms in his own house; but whoever is satisfied with the protection of the law is at liberty to sell his arms to the Government, which will receive them in part payment of arrears of revenue at a fair valuation.

* Friday is the holiest day of the Mahometan week ; and hence was appropriately selected for the market-day of the town of Bazaar ; for Bazaar was not only the chief town of Bunnoo, but the only public mart ; and it was resorted to both by the Bunnoochees of every tuppeh, and also by the various mountain tribes around the valley.   The former brought out their surplus produce, and the latter bartered their sheep, oxen, goats, wool, iron and salt, for corn, sugar, linen (from India), silks, arms, and gunpowder. It was essential that such a promiscuous assembly of friends and foes, all carrying three or four offensive weapons, should meet on some neutral ground ; and this was well found in that day of the week which Mahometans of every sect reverence alike.   I never myself witnessed a fair-day at Bazaar, but was informed that it was a most remarkable spectacle : seldom less than ten thousand wild Afghans, clad and armed in their different fashions, meeting in perfect peace, and exchanging the salutations enjoined by their common faith : ' Salâam Aleikoom !' 'Aleikoom Salâam !'   The day before, or the day after, they could not have met without a fight.

' 9. All duties on corn are henceforward abolished, as also all other cesses paid to the Mullicks of tuppehs, who will receive compensation after inquiry. Any Mullick convicted of levying duties from Hindūs, or others, will be severely fined, if not deposed.

' 10. Any Mullick, or peasant, who shall stop up the water, or cut away dams, so as either maliciously to dry up, or to flood the fields of his neighbours, shall be fined twice the amount of the damage so occasioned ; and the Mullicks of tuppehs, in particular, are held responsible for looking after the irrigation.

' 11. All lands that have been held for five years shall be confirmed to the holders, and all land disputes of a more recent date must be brought forward at once, when they will be settled by arbitration ; any not brought forward within six weeks after this proclamation will not be heard, except sufficient reason be shown, such as absence in a foreign country, or grievous sickness.

' 12. All Syuds, Oolumá, or other holders of hitherto *máfee* (rent-free) lands, will attend at the time of the revenue survey, and point out their lands; and when the extent of those lands has been ascertained by measurement, they must within twenty days after the said measurement give in to the

Nazim or Kárdár a written statement of the said lands, with the *sunnuds* (title-deeds, grants, etc.) or other authority by which they are held ; and when all these claims shall have been given in, they will be considered collectively, with reference to the proportion they shall prove to bear to the whole produce of the valley, and individually with reference to the conduct of the parties. Such malcontents as the Syuds of Mumukhsheyl cannot expect kindness from the Government ; no claims for *dhurum-urth* (charitable) lands will be registered after twenty days from the revenue survey.

' 13. Any zumeendar, Syud, or other holder of land who shall run away to escape payment of revenue, his lands and property shall be considered forfeited thereby to Government, which shall either sell the same or give them to well-wishers on mere payment of the arrears.

' 14. Any tuppeh which shall harbour revenue defaulters, or other public offenders, shall be held responsible for the claims against such persons ; and any Mullick who does not give speedy information of such persons being concealed within his jurisdiction will be removed forthwith.

' 15. The crimes of *suttee* * (widow burning), in-

* I do not know whether the Bunnoochees permitted the Hindūs who resided amongst them to burn their widows ; but think they would

fanticide and slave-dealing are forbidden under the severest penalties.

' 16. The system of *bégáree* (forced labour) will not be allowed either to Government officials, Mullicks, or any one else.

' 17. The manufacture of arms and gunpowder is forbidden, under penalty of five hundred rupees.

have done so on payment of a fee, if the Hindūs had been sufficiently strict in their observances to desire it. At any rate, in publishing laws *de novo* in a new country where there was a Hindū community, it was necessary and proper to infuse into those laws the spirit which the humane Colonel Lawrence had already introduced in the Punjāb, and persuaded Maharajah Goolab Singh, for his own credit among the English, to introduce in the kingdom of Cashmere. And I may here remark, that when English readers hear or read of the unpopularity of British rule in the East, it is well that they should know that by far the greatest share of this unpopularity arises from such interferences as these with the barbarous prejudices of the natives. The Hindū no longer feels himself a person of vital importance in his own house. His death will not shorten the days of his young wife., She will not adorn his funeral pile, nor her screams give solemnity to his exit from the world. She will happily survive as long as her Maker intended, and regret her lord only if he treats her well. Far be it from me to insinuate that if he treats her ill, his curry may even disagree with him ! The Mahometan feels equally aggrieved by these benevolent rulers. He also is now obliged to treat his wife as a woman should be treated, lest she presume to seek a kinder home ; in which case (so low has liberty fallen), he cannot kill her without being hanged !

Neither may either Hindū or Mahometan buy girls any longer by the pound ; nor those sacred races who cannot degrade themselves by giving their daughters in marriage to meaner men, be permitted any more to strangle them. In short, British rule has undoubtedly deprived the natives of many of the most valued luxuries of life. It has protected woman from man : and that great reformation is as odious as it is honourable.

'18. All weights and measures used by dealers in Bunnoo must assimilate to those in use at Lahore, and none will be allowed to be used which have not been stamped by the Kárdár, under penalty of a fine for each offence.

(Dated)
'Camp, Duleepgurh, Bunnoo.
'December 21st, 1847.'

*January 3rd*, 1848.—The arbitrators I appointed have settled the great land dispute in Jhundookheyl, between Sher Must and Swahn Khan ; and I this day bound the parties, under heavy penalties, to abide by their decision ; then packed them all off to mark out the boundary at once, before more doubts arise. Thus, by the influence of a dis-interested European, in whom both sides could trust, two very large estates, which had lain waste for several years, were brought back to fertility and use. I was amused by the choice of umpires. The Vizeeree chose three of his own nation, fearless of jealousy or foul play. The Bunnoochee could not trust his own people, and chose three low Mahometans out of the town of Bazaar—two oilmen and a gardener !

*January 4th.*—The reader will remember, that the foundation of the fort of Duleepgurh was laid on December 18th, 1847, so that the soldiers had now been labouring at it seventeen days.* They had been assisted also by some hundreds of coolies from the eastern bank of the Indus; and altogether there could scarcely have been less than four thousand men constantly at work, allowing for those absent on duty in the camp. Since the mutiny had been put down in Mân Sing's regiment the works had gone on with great rapidity. The earth to build the walls was dug out of the ditch, and there moistened, and made into mud, by a canal, and regulated by the workmen themselves. The soldiers, stripped to their blue *paijá-muhs*, divided themselves into gangs, and, standing at equal distances, kept up a constant rivalry as to which gang did the most. One grenadier would be seen down in the ditch filling an osier basket, or (failing that) his own shield, with well-trodden mud; another handing it, when full, to his comrade above the ditch, who tossed it to a third upon the wall, who threw it out where it was wanted, and passed down again the empty vehicle for more.

Here and there stood a corporal, or a sergeant, acting as overseer; and whenever he saw a

* I have omitted the account of the suppression of mutiny in one Sikh regiment which refused to work, because it was too interesting in itself, and would have diverted the reader's mind from our essential subject.—J. R.

superior approaching, shouted in a commanding tone, 'Get on! get on!' On the corner bastions (now rising into importance) perched the Colonels and Commandants, shaded by their immense *chattuhs* (umbrellas) of gay-coloured silks. From this high altitude they overlooked the busy scene, and encouraged their begrimed and toiling men, with witty remarks upon their awkwardness, sneers at the slower progress of the regiment next them, or (if no tell-tale was near to listen) sarcastic congratulations upon the dignity to which they had all arrived, in being promoted to bricklayers, after so many years' service in the inferior capacity of soldiers! A little before sunset, General Cortlandt and I would go out and dismiss the men to their dinners, and then walk round and survey the day's work, followed by all the gay umbrellas, which descended with their owners from the bastions at our arrival. Commendations to the zealous, and reproofs to the lazy, were then distributed in the hearing of all, and having seen the outside picket take up its post in advance of the fort, to prevent mischief during the night, we returned to camp, and left the deserted and silent works to be disturbed only by the measured footfall of the sentry.

The soldiers thus watched, and excited to

emulation, had raised the walls of the inner fort, by January 4th, to such a height as to form a complete and almost impregnable intrenched position, wherein to leave half the force and all the baggage, if necessity called out the other half.

At length, therefore, the moment had arrived to attempt the only really hazardous part of our enterprise, which the capitulation of the Vizeerees had left unfinished. I mean the levelling of the Bunnoochee forts.

That night was an anxious one to me, and I sat up hour after hour considering and reconsidering our position and means, and the best course for us to pursue. Again and again I thought over the opinion of the Acting-Resident, that the razing of the forts should be done by us, not thrown on the people; and that 'when the Sikh fort was ready, I should begin gradually to dismantle those of the most turbulent.' But I always came to the conclusion that he would not have given that advice had he ever seen the Bunnoochees, and known their irritable temper, and dislike to the intrusion of Sikh soldiers into the villages and among their women. He thought that my plan would unite the whole peasantry against us; and I thought the same of his! But then (as was ever the considerate custom of both

himself and Colonel Lawrence, with their assistants), after giving his advice, he left me to act
on my own discretion, fully confident that his
object was mine, and every nerve would be
strained to accomplish it. I did, therefore, what
I think an officer should always do when called
upon to act on his own responsibility—viz., act
also on his own judgment.

During the night I prepared the following proclamation, and issued it next morning.

### ' PROCLAMATION

#### ' TO THE BUNNOCCHEES AND VIZEEREES OF BUNNOO.

' A royal fort is, as you see, now being built by
the Lahore Sirkar in Bunnoo, and it has been called
Duleepgurh, in honour of the Maharajah.

' In it will remain four regiments of infantry, two
troops of horse artillery, fifty zumbooruhs, and one
thousand cavalry.

' This force is sufficient both to keep you in order
and to protect you against your enemies ; and as
you are forbidden by the laws which I before
published to have recourse to arms and fight among
yourselves, it is no longer necessary that every
village should be a fort.

' Where just laws are in force, every fakeer's hut

is a castle, because no one dare enter it to injure him.

'You are hereby ordered, therefore, to throw down to the ground the walls of every fort and enclosed village within the boundaries of Bunnoo; and I hold the Mullicks responsible for the carrying out of this order within fifteen days.

'At the end of fifteen days I will move against the first fort I see standing, considering the inhabitants as enemies, and remove every Mullick who has a fortification left in his tuppeh.

'The seed-time is over, and you have nothing to do in your fields. Let the Mullicks, therefore, of each fort collect the inhabitants and knock down their own walls, so that at the end of a fortnight the villages of Bunnoo may be open, like the villages of Murwut, Tâk, Esaukheyl, and other peaceful countries.

(Dated)
'Camp, Duleepgurh,
    5th January, 1850.'

# CHAPTER V.

## *THE FORTS FALL.*

*January 5th*, 1848.—This morning was published the proclamation for knocking down forts, and this evening Lal Baz Khan, of Bazaar, came to beg for a few more days over and above the fifteen allowed for the work of destruction, as his town and surrounding fortifications are more extensive than any one else's. The request, being reasonable, was granted, and he promised to begin razing to-morrow.

On this chief I always calculated to set the example, and hoped others would follow. None, however, came forward to-day.

But the next day, and the day after that, several pretty little things happened, to understand which I must here quote a previous entry of December 28th, as follows :—

' *December 28th, Camp, Dulcepgurh.*—Last night received an *urzee* (petition) from some chiefs in the Meerce tuppchs, to the effect that the Bukkykheyl

Vizeerees have again cut off some irrigation of theirs, which by my orders was opened some days ago. As the seed-time is now closing, this is a serious matter to the Meerees, so I determined to go in person and see the Vizeeree dam. Accompanied by General Cortlandt, Sirdar Mohammed Khan, Sirdar Ram Singh Chappehwalluh, and about one hundred and fifty horse, I set off early for the Meeree tuppehs. There I found an extensive plain, barren for want of water; and crossing the bed of the Tochee river, entered another great tract, which stretches away to the western hills, and is by right of seizure and possession the property of the Bukkykheyl Vizeerees. Their green, well-watered corn-fields presented a striking contrast with the dried-up acres of the poor Meerees, though the land of the latter was the best. No inquiry was needed. The two banks of the Tochee told their own tale. Pursuing the course of that river upwards, we came at last to the point where the stream should by right be divided, and go half to the Meerees and half to the Vizeerees. Here we found a strong new *bund* (dam), extending upwards of two hundred yards, completely preventing any water from flowing towards the Meerees, and conducting the whole stream of the Tochee to the lands of Bukkykheyl. Not a Vizeeree showed, but they were all close by in the hills. The first thing we did, therefore, was to crown the high stony hillocks, beneath which the dam lay, to prevent surprise ; and I then set half of the escort to work, with their hands and spears, to break down the dam, which was partly effected in about two hours. We then set fire to the brushwood pulled out of the dam, so as to prevent its reconstruction, and satisfied with seeing the whole Tochee now rushing down towards the Meerce tuppehs, we left our bonfire blazing, and retired, but did not reach camp till 3 p.m. To-morrow I shall send a party of sappers and miners mounted behind as many horsemen, to complete the destruction of the dam, and prevent the Bukkykheylees from having any more water till the Meerees have done sowing. The Meerce chiefs seeing the water coming down to their villages, mounted and galloped up, full of thanks—which were sincere enough, I dare say.

*January 6th.*—A thing occurred to-day, which I know not whether to ascribe to good feeling or fear. The Meeree chiefs have sent deputies of their own, along with others from their enemies the Bukkykheyl Vizeerees, to say that, through my interference (on 28th December), in breaking down the Vizeeree dam, on the Tochee river, they have now sown all their lands, and if I had no objection, the Vizeerees were welcome to a fair share of the water from this time. Both deputies said that the Meerees and Vizeerees have now come to an amicable agreement; and under the influence of fear (the Vizeerees of me, and the Meerees of the Vizeerees), I trust they will get on in future without squabbling, and cultivate their opposite sides of the river without firing at each other across the stream.

These interferences were the bright spots of my wild and laborious life. The peace that ensued came home to so many, and the cultivation it permitted sprang up and flourished so rapidly under that genial sun, that one's good wishes seemed overheard by better angels, and carried out upon the spot before charity grew cold. And, indeed, this is the great charm of civil employment in the the East. The officer who has a district under his charge has power to better the condition of many thousands; and the social state of the people is so simple, that his personal influence affects it as rapidly as the changes of the air do the thermometer.* In England the best men can scarcely hope to see their seed come up. Even charity is organized away out of the hands of individuals. A well-

___

* I should have liked to put all this paragraph in italics; but whenever Sir Herbert speaks on the general principles of political and charitable action, all he says, or ever said, should be put in italics.—J. R.

dressed secretary turns the handle of a mill, into which rich men throw guineas at one end, while poor men catch halfpence at the other. Sometimes the guineas come out blankets and coals instead of halfpence, but the machinery is the same; and the giver and the receiver never see each other's faces, and feel sympathy and gratitude only in the abstract.

*January 7th.*—The umpires in the land-dispute between Swahn Khan and Sher Must have returned, after laying down the mutual boundaries and building pillars upon them. The disputed tract (named Sudurawan) is itself nearly half a tuppeh, and both sides are delighted to bring it back to cultivation. As an illustration of the sort of justice which best suits these rude people, I must tell the reader that a branch of this great dispute referred to a small property called Oozjhdoo, which Sher Must had sold to Swahn Khan, and which he was now to get back again on refunding the purchase-money. The question arose, what *was* the purchase-money? Sher Must (who had to repay it) said three hundred and twenty rupees; but Swahn (who was to receive) said one thousand and twenty! Neither would abate a fraction, and the whole quarrel was as far as ever from a settlement, for the sake of this one point. 'Now,' said I, 'look here! One thousand

and twenty added to three hundred and twenty, equal one thousand three hundred and forty, and the half of that is six hundred and seventy, or the medium between both your statements. I shall take two pieces of paper, and write on one "six hundred and seventy," and on the other "three hundred and twenty," and then put them into my foraging-cap, and Sher Must shall pay whichever he draws out. Do you agree?' 'Agreed! agreed! That is true justice.* In destiny there is nothing wrong. God will do as he likes!' The foraging-cap was mysteriously shaken, and presented to Sher Must, who trembled violently as he put in his hand; and though he drew forth the most unfavourable figure, he was quite relieved when the solemn ordeal was over. Neither of the parties would have presumed to say a word against a decision thus pronounced, whatever they might have thought of one delivered by the Supreme Council of India.

*January* 10*th*.—Thinking it necessary to show the Bunnoochees that the order for knocking down their forts in fifteen days is not to be a dead letter, I this morning at sunrise rode out, accompanied by General Cortlandt and fifty horsemen, to see how the work of demolition was progressing; and pass-

---

* (*I* don't feel quite sure about that, Sir Herbert; and it seems to me the chance is dead against Swahn Khan.—J. R.)

ing down the right bank of the Khoorrum through the tuppehs of Bazaar and Moosch Khan, crossed over the river, and swept round through the four Sooraunee tuppehs on the left bank, reaching camp again at one o'clock.

The general progress is not great ; and, as usual, Lal Baz Khan of Bazaar, having most at stake, has set the best example. The order, however, has only been issued five days, and some of the Mullicks tell me they only got their copies of it yesterday. For the first day or two they all thought it was a joke, and tried to laugh at it as if it was a good one ; and when convinced by our serious manner that we were quite in earnest, they then began to look at each other, waiting to see what line of conduct their next neighbours would pursue. Such are the feuds among them, that more than one man has come forward to beg that his enemy may be made to knock his fort down first, or else it will be impossible for *him* to expose his village to an *enfilade*! In the midst of these conflicting feelings, the beloved stronghold stood intact ; but my visit of this morning has roused the people from their lethargy. If, as I approached a fort, the inhabitants jumped up on the walls, and began to make a show of levelling, I took it for granted they would obey, and passed on with a ' *Shábásh !* ' (Well done !) But three

forts that I came to were not inclined to render
so much homage ; they were closed and silent, and
it was as clear to be seen as if the walls were
glass that a proper set of rebels were inside. So I
quartered five horsemen upon each, and told them
not to come away without twenty rupees, and live
free and well till the fine was paid. Before noon
the chiefs of all three thought it better to pay the
fine, and get rid of their expensive visitors. To-
morrow I shall do the same in another direction,
and send parties all over the country to report
where work is going on and where it is not.

Among other forts, I visited two belonging to the
Vizeerces, on the edge of the Thull, and admirably
placed on a high bank surrounded on three sides by
a quicksand (in which the leader of our party was
nearly lost). I was greatly struck by observing
several Vizeerce horses out at graze on the open
plain. The instant they caught sight of us they
collected together, took a good long look at us to
make sure we were coming their way, and then
wheeling round, galloped off to their masters in the
forts, with as much judgment of what was proper
to be done under the circumstances as if they had
been Vizeeree sentinels.

*Bunnoochee horses similarly cast loose would use
their liberty only to fight, and run to any fort rather*

*than their master's.** So national is nature, and so strongly does the human master impress his own characters on his brute dependents.

The Vizeerees and Bunnoochees are both great breeders of horses; those of the former are remarkable for their good qualities and *curved ears*; those of the latter have beautiful legs, and are very active and hardy, *but so incurably vicious that they are only fit to be chained to the pole of a six-pounder gun, where lashing out behind is no inconvenience, and lying down impossible.*

*January* 12*th.*—To-day, being a great festival of the Sikhs, is a holiday for the whole force.

Rode out through the upper tuppehs of Bunnoo, and stirred up the activity of the peasantry in pulling down their forts; it makes both hands and hearts bleed. Paid a visit also to the forts of the Momundkheyl Vizeerees, who possess a fertile little island at the head of the Khoorrum, and contrary to the custom of all other Vizeerees, live the whole year in Bunnoo. Being quite in a corner, they thought to pass unobserved, and had not pulled down any part of their fortifications; but the

---

* I have italicised *this*, and the presently following sentences, being myself under the clearest conviction that half the powers and virtues of animals are unknown, and that two-thirds of their vices are our own. Also that the way to know their virtues is not by vivisection.—J. R.

moment we appeared in sight, it was amusing to see how rapidly they jumped astride the walls and began hammering away. The chiefs, too, rushed out, dragging a fat *doombuh* (sheep) as a *nuzzur* (offering). This, by-the-bye, is the universal offering of Bunnoo, and I never pass by a fort that I have not to refuse a sheep!

One fort which we visited to-day was entirely inhabited by Hindūs,—a singular instance in all Bunnoo. It is called 'Moolluh's Gurhee.' Now that this among other forts must come down, the Hindūs, afraid of living in an open village, have applied to be admitted into our new town of Duleepshuhr, the foundations of which are to be laid to-morrow.

*January* 13*th*.—Mullick Swahn Khan, Vizeeree, came to beg for a little delay in knocking down his fort, as all his people are engaged in ploughing and sowing the lands which have been just assigned to him by the umpires. As crops are more important than castles, I allowed him ten days more than the fifteen fixed originally.

By this time the whole population of the valley was engaged in demolishing the forts, for fear of being fined ; and I confess I viewed the progress of the work with equal shares of satisfaction and contempt. Had my proclamation been sent back

7

to me as gun-wadding, and the unanimous chiefs
shut themselves up in their forts and defied me to
pull them down, the valley of Bunnoo, for aught I
know, might have been free at this moment. To
be sure, it would have been a hell; but what of
that? the Bunnoochees liked it.

Having ascertained that the chiefs of a tribe of
Vizcerees, named Janeekheyl, who hold lands adjoining those of Bukkykheyl, on the east of Bunnoo,
have never come in to me, nor signed the Vizeeree
agreement, and that the whole tribe is now in the
hills, I have sent through Swahn Khan to inquire
if they mean to stay where they are? If so, I
will give their lands to other people. If not, they
had better come and sign the agreement.

A great number of the Hindūs of Bunnoo
having come to beg that places may be allowed
them in the new capital, I walked over with them
to the spot, where the streets are now being laid
out, and asked them what they thought of the plan.
It was generally approved, but every one made a
special request that *his* particular house might be
the nearest to the fort! Already the applications
are so numerous, that we have been obliged to
extend our plan; and it is probable that the trade,
not only of this rich valley, but also of Esaukheyl,
Murwut Tâk, and Kolächee, will soon centre in

Duleepshuhr, instead of, as hitherto, in Dera Ishmael Khan. That town, indeed, when I saw it last, was in a very decayed condition ; and I am assured that one natural obstacle exists to its ever becoming a very prosperous settlement : the white ants are so destructive, that it is impossible to keep a store of grain in the town ; and for the daily consumption of the inhabitants, supplies are brought in from the country, and across the Indus. When General Cortlandt arrived, and inspected the fort of Ukálgurh at Dera, he found the greater part of the grain in store quite pulverized by white ants.

*January* 14*th.*—Some Meeree chiefs came in to beg that I would allow half the height of one of their largest forts to remain standing, as the fort is directly under the hills of their enemies, the Vizeerees, and absolutely necessary as a city of refuge. They also interceded for another fort, which commands their irrigation. These requests seem reasonable, but I shall ride out myself to-morrow morning to the spot, and see that they are true ; for I hold the levelling of the forts to be the key-stone of the subjugation of Bunnoo, and will let off none that I can help.

*January* 15*th.*—This morning, according to pro-mise, galloped out to the Meeree border, and, after inspection, gave permission for the walls of two forts, named Noorár and Shuheedán, to be left standing, as high as a man could reach with his hand. (Of course they will pick out a big fellow to measure with !)

Was pleased, indeed, to see that a great portion of the lately barren plain of the Mecrees has been sown since I released the irrigation from the Vizeerees ; but still it came too late to plough and sow the whole.

*January* 16*th.*—This evening I received all the officers of the force, and called upon them to enforce the camp regulations against soldiers going out alone, and remaining out after sunset. They proposed to lay a counter-ambush near the mill, to shoot the Bunnoochees who lurk there at night ; but though the chances are, ninety-nine out of a hundred, that they would shoot the right persons, yet there is one chance that they might shoot the wrong. Besides, there is something repugnant in taking a man's life out of a hiding-place, before he has, by any overt act, discovered hostile intentions.

I also took the opportunity of remarking on the wantonness of destroying mulberry-trees for firewood—a practice which the soldiers are getting into, now that they feel themselves a little secure in their new country, and which has already disgraced the Sikh armies so shamefully in Cashmere and Peshawur.

There is plenty of wood to be purchased, if the men will only encourage the peasants to bring it in, by buying, instead of stealing it. At Cashmere, the Sikh soldiers very nearly cleared away the poplars, and did much injury to the chunár, or plane-trees,* and the valley of Peshawur was almost denuded of the mulberry, once so plentiful and valuable. The wantonness of all soldiers is very great in the way of plundering supplies of all sorts, if good discipline be not observed in the army to which they belong ; for they are birds of passage, and feel that they will not miss to-morrow the shade of the grove which they injure to-day. But though I have seen a soldier of Hindūstan pull the door off an empty house to cook a chupattee with, I do not think the same man would have cut down a graceful poplar, or plane-tree, for he would have been too civilized, and felt the enormity of the act.

---

* Mr. Vigne, the enterprising traveller in Cashmere, saw on the spot what I have merely heard of from others. He says : " A great number of these fine trees have been destroyed by the Sikhs. The Governor, Mihan Singh, cut down some in the Shálimár, and sold them ; but Runjeet ordered him to repair the damage as well as he could ! In the times of the Pathāns no man could cut down a chunár under a penalty of five hundred rupees, even on his own ground."—Vigne's ' Travels in Kashmīr,' vol. ii., p. 95.

A Sikh, on the contrary, has no feeling on such a subject—no love of nature. He sees no aspirations in the towering of the cypress, no sadness in its bending before the wind ; he views it with the eye of a carpenter, and would tell you to a foot how long it would last him and his comrade for fire-wood. In the forest of Lebanon I believe he would sit down and chop four new legs for his bed ; for it is a well-known fact that the Sikh soldiers pulled the roof off a palace of Rajah Heera Singh's at Jusrotuh for no other purpose than to get the beams, which were of a favourite wood, for bed-steads.

The reader will remember that I gave the Bunnoochees fifteen days wherein to raze their forts. At the end of that time many came to me and deprecated my being angry, or fining them for not fulfilling their task in the appointed time, declaring that they had done their best, and appealing to the very great progress they had made. I was indeed quite content with their labours, but made a great favour of extending their days of grace. Twenty days had now elapsed, and about two-thirds of the destruction was accomplished.

In the whole of Bunnoo there may be now twenty or thirty uninhabited forts whose walls are still standing intact, there being no one to knock them down. Of the rest, I should say two hundred are already level with the ground, one hundred down as low as a man's waist, and seventy or eighty as high as a man. The fact is, that the demolition is no easy work. The mud is like iron, and the Bunnoochees hate labour as cordially as all other Puthán.

So here I shall bring this long chapter to a close; and as the springing up of a great war at the opposite end of the Indus too soon overwhelmed these peaceful labours (if, indeed, they may be called peaceful, in virtue of the end they had in view), and prevented me from ever again returning to Bunnoo, let me ask the kind reader to review, for a moment, in his own mind, the chapters which he has read, and consider whether enough of peril, enough of anxiety and responsibility, enough of wild adventure and barbarian life, and if not enough of accomplishment, at least of good endeavour, were crowded into these first three months of my 'Year upon the Punjáb Frontier.'

On the 9th of December, 1847, we entered Bunnoo.

On the 17th of the same month, the powerful, brave, and hitherto unconquered Vizeeree tribes resigned their independence, and consented to pay tribute ; and, as far as I know, and with such occasional exceptions as any one might suppose, have abided by that agreement till this day.

On the 18th of December was laid the foundation of the royal fort of Duleepgurh ; and, in spite of the mutiny of one of the regiments, that structure was raised by the hands of the Sikh army, under my command, to the height of twenty feet, or within six feet of the top, before I left Bunnoo, on the 28th of February, 1848, or in the short space of seventy-two days. And this, in an enemy's country, without an engineer, and almost without tools.

On the 5th of January, 1848, the people and chiefs of Bunnoo were ordered to throw down their forts, about four hundred in number.

By the end of a month, in spite of being preached against in the mosques, in spite of two open attempts at assassination, and a third plot to murder me in a gateway, I had carried that measure out, and left but two Bunnoochee forts standing in the valley, and those two by my permission.

Such were the chief results which had been accomplished by this expedition in less than three months ; but besides these, a new town had been

founded, which, at this day, is flourishing; a
military and commercial road, thirty feet broad
and twenty-five miles long, had been undertaken,
laid down, commenced, and has since been completed, through a formerly roadless valley, and is
now (under the protection of ordinary police)
traversed by the merchant and traveller in ease
and security; tracts of country from which the
fertilizing mountain streams were diverted by lawless feuds, had been brought back to cultivation
by the protection of a strong Government; others
lying waste, because disputed, had been adju-
dicated, apportioned, occupied, and sown once
more; through others, a canal had been de-
signed and begun, and promised to create a
fruitful country in a desert; while, still nearer
approaching to civilization, a people who had
worn arms as we wear clothes, and used them
as we use knives and forks, had ceased to carry
arms at all; and though they quarrelled still,
learnt to bring their differences to the bar of
the civil court, instead of the sharp issue of the
sword.

In a word, the valley of Bunnoo, which had
defied the Sikh arms for five-and-twenty years,
had in three months been *peacefully* annexed to
the Punjāb, and two independent Afghan races,

the Vizeerees and the Bunnoochees, *been subjugated without a single shot being fired.*

I believe I may add, that under the firm, yet benevolent, administration of my successor, Major Reynell Taylor, there is at this moment no part of the Punjāb where there is less crime, and more security, than in BUNNOO.

END OF PART I.

# PART II.

## THE SHORES OF INDUS.

---

## CHAPTER I.

### *THE STORY OF SHAH NIWAZ OF TÁK.*

AMIDST the various civil business transacted by Lieutenant Edwardes during his expedition to Bunnoo, two very interesting passages occurred, of considerably more importance than the rest, determining, to the great advantage of their inhabitants, the princedoms of two fertile provinces lying between Bunnoo and the Indus— the provinces, namely, of Tâk and Esaukheyl.

Neither of them larger than an English midland shire, or French department, but, being in latitude 32°, and well watered—Tâk capable of artful irrigation, and Esaukheyl traversed by divided branches of the Indus—they had before Edwardes' time become each of them a little kingdom, Tâk having been made so because one of its first chiefs was a master of agriculture.

8

Tâk is the most northern country of the Dérajât, or plain of the Indus.

It has a branch of the Soolimânee range on the north ; the Vizeeree hills of the same range, on the west ; and it is irrigated by two hill streams, the Zam and the Gomul, whose waters have turned a barren plain and camel pasture into a fertile and highly cultivated country, during the last three generations. A third hill stream reaches it on the north-east ; whose waters, unlike those of the Zam and Gomul, are esteemed pure and wholesome to drink, but I am not aware that they contribute much to the cultivation.

Of these rivers the Gomul is the principal, and may well be called the parent of the present prosperity of the country. It emerges from the great Soolimânee range by the same pass as the Lohânee caravans, and it would naturally pursue its course between the inner and outer range of the lower hills which lie at the foot of the Throne of Solomon. But Surwur Khan, a former Lord of Tâk (of whom more by-and-by), threw an enormous dam across the Gomul, at Gwaleyree, diverted it into Tâk through the lands of the Meeances, who live at the mouth of the pass, and erected a fort to guard the same. Thus no portion of the Gomul reaches the Gundapoor

country, south of Tâk, except in seasons of flood,
when the overflow which escapes the Gwaleyree
dam takes its natural course, and comes down to
Koláchee, through the 'Red Pass.' So much of its
waters as enter Tâk are exhausted in its fields.

The country of Tâk, three generations ago,
would have been described only as the pasture
grounds of the tribe of Dowlutkheyl, whose old
head-quarters I believe still exist under the name
of 'Old Tâk,' three koss from the present capital ;
but the present extensive town of Tâk was founded
in a very humble manner by one Kuttál Khan,
(son of Zeman Khan, their hereditary chief), who
migrated from Old Tâk with about half a dozen
families of operatives, chiefly potters, and settled
where the mansion called Surwur, Khan's Huveylee
now stands.

One day, a potter's wife came and complained
to him that the people of Old Tâk had carried
off her mule, which she had taken to the river to
fetch water, and added, " My husband and I came
here at your invitation, and we rely on your
honour to protect us." Kuttál Khan, like a true
Afghan, swore great oaths not to eat or drink till
he had avenged her ; and, taking a handful of
men along with him, went out to Old Tâk, killed
the thieves, and brought back the mule.

The poor people of Old Tâk beheld this act
with admiration ; and, considering Kuttál a better
chief than his father to live under, they migrated
in large numbers to New Tâk, which soon contained one hundred shops of Hindū traders,
and about one thousand families of Hindūs and
Mohammedans together ; a change which the rest
of the Dowlutkheyl tribe looked on with jealousy,
but involuntary respect—for Kuttál was admitted
to be no ordinary Afghan.

* He at first assiduously courted popularity,
and persuaded the Dowlutkheyl to engage in the
reduction of some little tribes in their neighbour-
hood.

He was intrusted with the command, and thus
obtained a pretext for raising troops, which the
contributions of the Dowlutkheyl, and his exactions
from the conquered tribes, gave him the means
of maintaining.  By these means he collected
about three hundred Beloochees and Sindees, and
proceeded to build a fort ; after which he thought
himself secure, assumed the right to levy a revenue
from the public ryots, and began to tyrannize over
his own tribe.

---

* The next four pages are quoted by Sir Herbert from Mr. Elphinstone, but I cannot put inverted commas because I cut the sentences
about as suits my own subject, taking care not to alter their sense.

The tribe was at first struck with dismay, and submitted to his oppression ; till at length he openly assumed the character of a Sovereign, and ordered the people to pay their duty at his Court every morning. Two of the Mullicks, to whom he first proposed this homage, refusing to comply, Kuttál told them, that if they did not attend in the course of two mornings, their heads should be hung up over their own doors by the third.

The Mullicks withdrew, and hastily assembling the tribe and the ryots, pointed out Kuttál's designs, and engaged them in a conspiracy against him, which was confirmed by solemn oaths. Next morning the whole population assembled in arms, and besieged Kuttál in his fort. After a siege of three days, in which many people were killed, the water in the fort was exhausted, and the garrison was obliged to evacuate it, and Kuttál escaped on horseback, accompanied by some trusty attendants on foot. His flight was soon discovered, his enemies set off in all directions to pursue him, and eight of them took the road by which he was flying. His attendants were soon fatigued, and one man alone remained with him. Kuttál (says one of my informants) at this time wore a robe which was given him by a Dervise, and by the virtue of which he had obtained his present

greatness; in the precipitation of his flight this
robe fell off, and immediately his remaining
attendant became lame, and lagged behind: soon
after his pursuers appeared; Kuttál's courage
had left him with his robe, and he had recourse
to humble intreaties for mercy; some of his
pursuers answered that they were sworn, and others
that he had never shown mercy to them; and at
last one of them ran him through with a spear·
Kuttál's family were all seized. Gool Khan,
one of the principal conspirators, was put at the
head of the tribe, and thus was baffled the first
attempt at the subversion of the liberties of the
Dowlutkheyl.

Surwur Khan, the eldest son of Kuttál, was at
this time only sixteen, but he was well educated,
and endowed with great natural capacity. By the
assistance of his mother he effected his escape
from prison; and, by a train of reasoning which
could only have occurred to an Afghan, he was
led to go straight to Zuffer, the brother of Gool
Khan, and throw himself on his protection. He
reached this chief's house without discovery; and
Zuffer, in the true spirit of Afghan honour,
immediately resolved to protect him, even at the
risk of his brother's destruction. He accordingly
fled with him to the Murwut country, and soon

after began to intrigue at Cabul for assistance from the Court. Their intrigues were successful, and Abdoorcheem Khan was sent with four thousand men to restore Surwur to his father's office.

In the meantime, Gool Khan had begun to be heartily tired of his magistracy. The tribe had turned into a turbulent democracy, over which he exercised a precarious, yet invidious authority; and a sedition had broken out about the property left by Kuttál, which Gool Khan wished to appropriate to himself.

The Dowlutkheyl began to murmur at his government; and one of them had drawn his sword on him, and asked, 'if he thought they had killed Kuttál to make him their master?' He was, therefore, equally terrified at the prospect of Surwur's success, and at the continuance of the democracy; and heard with pleasure an overture from Surwur, which seemed to present the only safe retreat from his perilous situation. Accordingly, when Surwur approached, Gool Khan's management, supported by the terror of the royal arms, disposed the Dowlutkheyl to submit; and Surwur taking a solemn oath to forget past injuries, they consented to receive him as their chief. This appearance of forgiveness was kept up till all the

leading men had been got together, when eighteen
of them were seized and put to death. Gool
Khan was spared, but on a subsequent quarrel
Surwur put him also to death.

His government was now established ; all those
who could oppose him had been made away with,
and nobody in the tribe had the courage to rebel.
He continued to strengthen himself, and to put
the murderers of his father to death as they fell
into his hands ;—twelve years ago, all his enemies were extirpated, and his power was at its
height. Since then, he has governed with great
justice and moderation ; his steady and impartial
administration is popular among the ryots, but
odious to the Dowlutkheyl, whose independence it
restrains.

Thus far the story has been told by Mr. Elphinstone. Sir Herbert continues, after giving some
further details of the death of Kuttál, unnecessary
here :—" When Surwur Khan had thus repossessed
himself of the fort and government of Tâk, he set
vigorously to work to strengthen both ; collected
guns, soldiers, etc., and became a powerful independent prince. He was one of those men who
seem born to usurpation, and justify their mission
by using power for the benefit of mankind. His
creative genius could see future harvests on the

parched and thorny plain of Tâk; and he went up in arms to the hills, fought with the wild Vizeerees for the streams, and led the fertilizing waters down into his country. Thus the Dowlut-kheyl passed in his day from a pastoral to a cultivating people; as he imposed on them a mild revenue and just laws, they had no reason to regret the loss of their ancestral liberties; and certainly I can myself testify that they sincerely revere his memory, and make his acts and his laws the standard of excellence in government. Had he lived in the west instead of the east he would have been one of the most civilized princes of his day, for he had a passion for the beautiful as strong as his love of utility and right. He sent north, south, east, and west, for *trees and flowers of every kind, and planted them round his fort and city; and as formerly there was not a tree in Tâk, so now there was not one in all the east of which a specimen was not to be found here.*\* The luxurious private gardens of the fort were the abodes of the choicest slaves, and the common people still tell marvellous tales of the harem of Surwur Khan.

When the Cabul dynasty decayed, and the

---

\* Mr. Masson, who visited Tâk in 1826, says: "The approach to Tâk from the east is distinguished by an avenue of full-grown mimosas, extending perhaps three miles" (vol. i., p. 49).—*These have long since been cleared away by the Sikhs.*

sovereignty of the Déraját was usurped by the Nuwab of Dera Ishmael Khan, I am not aware that Surwur Khan ever submitted to his authority; and as he assumed the title of Nuwab himself, it is probable that the two never stood to each other in any other relation than that of rivals.

But the resources of the little province of Tâk were unequal to a contest with the " Lion of the Punjâb "; and when the Sikhs crossed the Indus and swept away the Nuwab of Dera, Surwur Khan showed his usual ability in tendering his submission and agreeing to pay tribute.

This tribute originally consisted of three thousand rupees, three horses, one pair of hawks, twenty-five camels, and eight hunting dogs; but three years after this was imposed, Runjeet Singh went in person across the Indus, and raised the Tâk tribute to sixty thousand rupees. The total revenue of the province under Surwur was 125,000 to 150,000 rupees. Surwur Khan knew well that he could not resist; and so long as he lived, saved himself from dishonour, and his people from oppression, by regularly paying what was imposed on him, so that the Sikhs had no excuse for sending a plundering army into Tâk.

When Surwur Khan died, he was succeeded by his eldest son, Alladad Khan, a voluptuary who carried all his father's love of pleasure to excess without inheriting his ability, or any other noble quality, save courage.

The Sikhs thought the time was come to raise the revenue of this tributary province; Alladad, lost in revelry, paid no heed to his affairs, fell into arrears, became refractory, and was crushed. He fled to the hills, and took refuge among the Vizeerees, either his mother or some other of his father's wives having been a daughter of that tribe; and the country of Tâk was given by Runjeet Singh as a jageer * to his own grandson, Nao Nihal.

Assisted by his Vizeeree relations, Alladad made such continual inroads into his former kingdom that he almost reduced it to the barrenness from which his father had raised it; and Nao Nihal, unable with his Sikh regulars and guns to come up with an enemy who descended by surprise and retreated as rapidly to the hills, threw up his jageer in disgust; and the Sikhs not knowing what else to do with it, made it a means of pensioning a few unoffending relatives and dependents of Surwur Khan, and three Afghan chiefs, who had been retainers of the Nuwab of Dera when he gave up his Trans-Indus country.

---

* Grant of freehold land.

In the winter of 1846, I was in the hills of Jummoo, upwards of three hundred miles from Tâk, when one morning my moonshee introduced two Puthâns, who, he said, were in distress. They were dressed in the commonest white clothing, and had an air of misery mingled with "ashamed to beg." They talked of places I had never heard of across the Indus, and of events of which I was ignorant; but I gathered that they had seen better days, and, without attending much to the story, gave them ten rupees between them. They took the money gratefully, and departed; and I saw them no more till February of the following year, 1847, when I was ordered to proceed in charge of the first expedition to Bunnoo.

Again my two Puthân petitioners appeared, and asked to be allowed to go with me, as their native country was also across the Indus, and they would fain visit their homes again, if they might do so under my protection. Moreover, their wives and families had taken refuge in Bunnoo, and perhaps they might be of service to me. I consented, and we all left Lahore together. On the march I naturally busied myself with seeking information about the countries we were going to; and during the heat of the day collected a knot of natives round me, in the shade of a tree, and learnt all

I could. It was in one of these conversations that our talk brought us to Tâk, and, with my finger on the map, I asked who knew anything about that country ? One of the two Puthâns modestly lifted up his head, and said : 'My father was once King of it ! ' It was indeed Shah Niwaz Khan, the son of that Alladad from whom the Sikhs had taken Tâk ; and grandson of that Surwur who had brought streams from the mountains to fertilize it, and turned its desert plain into a richly cultivated land.

As his tale unfolded, I thought of my miserable ten rupees at Jummoo, and felt deeply grieved at having given such paltry relief to such great misfortunes. On inquiry, I found he had had no food for two days, after selling his arms and a few remaining ornaments ; so I ordered him five hundred rupees out of the treasury, and sent him on rejoicing to Bunnoo, to see his exiled family and bring me tidings from the valley.

At the conclusion of the first expedition, Shah Niwaz accompanied me in my *détour* through Murwut, Tâk, and Dera Ishmael Khan, and thus caught a transient peep at the tall fort of his ancestors.

One of my duties was to inquire how the Sikh officials governed the provinces intrusted to them, and see what was the condition of the countries themselves. I found Tâk little more satisfactory in appearance than the countries under the immediate rule of Dowlut Raie ; but as few complaints were made to me by the people, I had no occasion to report more to the Resident at Lahore than that I could not see any signs of prosperity in the jageer of the Afghan chiefs. But it so happened that at this time great reductions were being made by the Lahore Council in the jageers of all the chiefs of the Punjâb (unless, perhaps, their own might be excepted !) to meet the exigencies of the State ; and one of the first things I heard on returning to Lahore was that the jageer of Tâk was to be resumed. The measure had been proposed by the Chancellor, Rajah Deena Nâth, though he was well known to be the chief patron of Dowlut Raie and his friends the Afghan chiefs. Greatly as I was astonished, I could find no clue to the mystery at that time ; and the Resident, hard pressed for finances, readily consented to see a lakh of rupees per annum transferred to Schedule A, and the foreigners who held it to Schedule B.

The question that succeeded was, what was to be done with Tâk ? I was then, and am still, of opinion that a people is almost always more justly ruled and better off under the British Government

than under their own native chiefs; but I was
equally of opinion, from my own personal observa-
tion, that a Mohammedan tribe is infinitely happier
under its own Khan, even if he be below par, than
under a bigoted Sikh official.    For this reason I had
double pleasure in procuring the restoration of the
chiefs of Esaukheyl, for I believed the change would
be no better for them than for the people ; and now
that Tâk was no longer to be a jageer, but to be
governed by a Sikh Kárdár, I unhesitatingly made
a similar recommendation, and begged the Resident
to give the charge to Shah Niwaz.    He would, it is
true, no longer be an independent prince like his
father, and he would have to collect revenue for the
Sikhs instead of for himself ; but it would make
him well off in worldly circumstances, it would
restore him to his home and country, and it would
place over the people a grandson of that Surwur
Khan whose memory was so dear to them, and
whose laws they were always regretting.

    That so sudden a turn of fortune would not
inspire Shah Niwaz with the hope of making himself independent, (a doubt which must arise, and
be well weighed in such a case,) I judged from his
disposition, which was humble almost to broken-
heartedness.

    The proposal pleased Sir Henry Lawrence, who

valued power only for the good it enabled him
to do ; and though the measure was vehemently
opposed by the Sikh Chancellor, who prophesied
a rebellion, and discountenanced even by the timid
Tej Singh, who went so far as to shake his head in
open council, poor Shah Niwaz Khan, who yesterday had no clothes, received a dress of honour
(not much moth-eaten), and was dispatched with
a bounding and grateful heart to administer the
government of his native country.*

The terms on which he received it were these :—
The revenue of Tâk was estimated at one hundred
thousand rupees a-year, of which he was to pay
seventy-five thousand to the Sikh treasury and keep
twenty-five thousand for his own maintenance and
civil expenses. The Crown was to pay the garrison
and repairs of the fort. This arrangement was to
be at first only for one probationary year ; during

---

* During the war of 1848-9, when the Mooltanee Putháns did
better service as soldiers than they had ever done as governors of
country, they disclosed to me the reason both of their removal from
Tâk by Deena Náth, and that official's opposition to the appointment
of Shah Niwaz. The Chancellor calculated that when they were
reduced to despair by losing their jageer, they would pay handsomely
to recover it : a golden prospect unexpectedly marred by Shah Niwaz
getting it for nothing ! I am afraid the ousted Mooltanees to this day
think I also recommended their removal, in order to restore Shah
Niwaz. But I only availed myself of the opening ; I neither made it,
nor hoped for it.

which, if the Khan gave satisfaction, the lease was
to be renewed "during good behaviour."

This took place in the summer of 1847. Six
months afterwards I returned to Bunnoo with the
second expedition, and during the whole of my
stay in those parts I never had but two complaints
brought against the young Khan, and both were
frivolous; while the whole country (not only of
Tâk, but the adjacent valleys) was full of his good
report. Tâk at his accession had been on the
verge of ruin. The Afghan chiefs had screwed the
people till they abandoned their lands and went
elsewhere; and when they received the tidings of
their removal, they put the very water of the river
up for sale to the cultivators, and when these refused
to purchase, turned the stream into the ditch of
the fort of Tâk, and wasted it rather than let it feed
the poor. A more wanton and iniquitous act of
tyranny never came under my notice—even across
the Indus. Shah Niwaz recalled the fugitive cultivators of his tribe; restored the revenue laws of
his grandfather, Surwur Khan; sat daily in his
own durbar, and transacted his own affairs with an
ability for which none had given him credit, and
which required no assistance from middlemen; and,
in short, so ruled the country which had been
intrusted to him, that it prospered and was happy.

9

I will mention one amusing instance of Shah Niwaz Khan's reforms, before passing to other topics.

At the same time that he was appointed to the charge of Tâk, General Van Cortlandt was appointed to supersede Dewan Dowlut Raie in the government of the whole province of Dera Ishmael Khan. Shah Niwaz, therefore, accompanied his superior as far as Dera, on arrival at which place they heard that Tâk was in a state of siege. The Afghan Jageerdars, so often mentioned, and now about to be removed, had made prisoners of two Vizeerees from the adjacent mountains, and endeavoured, by pouring hot water on the muscles of their arms, and other barbarous tortures, to extract a heavy ransom from them or their friends. The prisoners found means to convey intelligence of their situation to the tribe ; and the enraged Vizeerees rose, and descended. into the plains to attack Tâk and liberate their countrymen.

At this juncture General Cortlandt arrived at Dera, and the beleaguered Jageerdars of Tâk called on him to assist them and save the town from plunder. The General consulted with Shah Niwaz, who finally undertook to draw off the Vizeerees if the two prisoners were given up to him—a negotiation in which he at once succeeded.

But this was not all. Shah Niwaz found among the mountain host a band of outlaws from his own country, who had formerly been his father's soldiers, and on that account expelled by the Jageerdars. These men revenged and fed themselves by such constant forays across the border that they became the dread of the country. If ever they caught a Kuthree trader on the road, they put him up behind them on a saddle, and bumped him off to the Vizeeree hills, whence they made him write for a ransom suitable to the state of his business, sometimes not less than one thousand rupees. At the time I speak of, no Hindū dare go out of his village.

The leader of this daring gang was a man named Peera. Shah Niwaz took off the ban of outlawry, and invited him to return to Tàk, pardoned of all past offences, if he would lead an honest life for the future. Peera joyfully agreed ; and bidding a rude farewell to the Vizeerees who had sheltered him in his misfortune (among whom he distributed eighty camels he had lately driven away from the plains !) he mounted the faithful mare, to whose fleetness and endurance he had often owed his life, and rode into Tàk as proudly as any Consul for whom a triumph was waiting in the streets of Rome. Nor went he without his greeting.    The people of the city flocked out to meet him, and dancers and musicians led the way to his ancient hovel.    Trays of sweetmeats were there presented him, a citizens dinner smoked under his unaccustomed nose, the high-bred mare, all skin and bone from her long marches, was rubbed down and caressed by admiring boys and girls ; and all night long, under the bright moon, the most beautiful dancers of Tâk strove who should win most smiles from the repentant outlaw. So great was the people's terror of him while abroad, and joy at his adopting the pursuits of peace.

It was a series of such acts as this that made the appointment of Shah Niwaz Khan a blessing to the country of Tâk.

# CHAPTER II.

ESAUKHEYL is a slip of country about forty miles long, which lies parallel with the Indus, having the great salt mines of Kálábágh on the north, the Khyssore range on the south, and the Salt range on the west. On the east the mighty Indus used to be its boundary, but in justice cannot be termed so any longer.

The Indus pursues its course with the sagacity of a living thing. Burning with all the zeal of the Mohammedan races on its banks to perform its pilgrimage, it seems, from its high altitude in Tibet, to have scanned the map of Central Asia, and discerned that it was nearer to the Indian Ocean than the Caspian. In vain the Indian Caucasus, seeking a bridegroom for her daughter Oxus, stands across its path : it detects an opening, and rushes by. In vain the Soolimánee range stretches out its arms to draw it into the thirsty vales of Afghanistan : it leaps through the rocks of Attock and Kálábágh, and takes refuge in the sandy deserts of the south, nor resumes its western course till the Mountains of

Solomon are passed, when it turns with its fellow-traveller the Sutlej ; and the two, with loud songs, as of pilgrims whose place of pilgrimage is in sight, roll on uninterruptedly to the sea.

The Indus has for many years been gradually taking a more westernly course in its passage to the Sutlej, and nowhere perhaps so markedly as at Esaukheyl. Here, year after year, it has encroached on the western bank, and in removing from the Sindh Sàgur has increased its breadth of terra firma. The alluvium thus thrown up has in process of time created on the left, or eastern bank, a low, but highly fertile tract called Kuchee.

At Meanwallee, the point where you leave the Sindh Sàgur Doâb to cross over to Esaukheyl, the Doâb of Sindh Sàgur is now no longer discernible from the ferries of Esaukheyl.

It was impossible for the Afghans of Esaukheyl to see twelve miles of the breadth of their country quietly transferred to the people of the Punjâb ; and when Ahmud Khan (elder brother of Mohammed Khan, the present chief) was at their head, they brought the men of Kuchee to an understanding, and caused a mutual boundary to be laid down in Kuchee on the eastern bank, parallel with the Indus, the Sindh Sàgur, and Esaukheyl.

In the confusion of the Punjâb kingdom, and the

jealousies ever existing between the Sikh Governors of neighbouring districts, Ahmud Khan's boundary was but ill observed ; and the land, not being needed by the oppressed Esaukheylees, became covered with a high jungle of reeds, tiger-grass, and tamarisk.

I have heard old Khalsa soldiers say, that when Runjeet Singh first came this way—probably when he went to Lukkee, in Murwut—he opened a way through this jungle for his army, by putting four elephants abreast, and making them go on in front, crushing. tearing down, and trampling into a highway, the undisturbed vegetation of years.

The residence of a British Agent at the Lahore Court, from the year 1846, very soon gave a new value to land and impulse to cultivation, by establishing every man's rights and securing to him his gains ; and Sir Henry Lawrence still further promoted industry by proclaiming that all land newly brought into cultivation, without prejudice to older land, should be rent-free for three years.

Amongst others, the Esaukheylees wished to extend their cultivation, by breaking up their jungle-covered alluvium, on the opposite bank of the river ; and many were the formal notices filed in General Cortlandt's court, of their intention to embark capital, on the faith of the Resident's term of grace.

But the men of Kuchee thought the history of

their mushroom country was already old enough to
be forgotten, and they claimed the whole of the new
land between the high bank of the old Sindh Sâgur
and the Indus.    " There was not a child," they said,
" so ignorant as not to know that Esaukheyl was on
the *right* bank of the Indus ! "

After hearing both sides, I thought the face of
the country, with which I was myself familiar,
decided clearly enough in favour of the men of
Esaukheyl ; and I ordered the elders of that country,
with their chief and Government Kárdár, to go over
to Kuchee, meet the elders and authorities on a
certain day, and formally retrace the boundary of
Ahmud Khan.

The Kárdár of Kuchee, a true Sikh official, named
Rám Singh, instead of obeying his orders, and tracing
the old boundary, allowed his clients—the men of
Kuchee—to re-open the whole question, and start,
*de novo*, with the protest that their boundary was
the Indus, flow where it might.

The expression they used on this occasion, was
that the Indus was a " hud-i-Secundur," or Alex-
andrian boundary ; of which, as I had never heard
before, I asked the meaning, and was informed
that they did not intend to say that Alexander the
Great had decided the Indus to be their boundary,
but that *the Indus was an Alexander in its own*

*peculiar way*, dividing lands as it thought proper, and giving them to whom it chose, by fiats which could neither be disputed nor resisted.

The plea was too poetical for our purpose, which was eminently practical ; and, if admitted, would have left the Esaukheylees the prospect of soon having no country at all. So I fined Rám Singh fifty rupees for thinking when he ought to have obeyed, and left the boundary of Ahmud Khan to be retraced by General Cortlandt.

The tale of Shah Niwaz of Esaukheyl, as it is given by Sir Herbert in sequel of this description of his country, is even more eventful than that of Surwur Khan and his grandson, and if I had space to follow it in detail, would be a curious example of the persistent adversity—as Surwur Khan's of the favour of Fortune. But the tale of Esaukheyl is too much entangled with the history of Runjeet Singh himself to be abstracted in any intelligible simplicity ; and I am compelled, therefore, to give only the concluding passages of it, which bear on the circumstances of the campaign of Kineyree.

In the days of Runjeet Singh, the chiefs of Esaukheyl had been always hospitable and attentive to British officers—long before the wisest seer could have foretold the annexation of the Punjáb to British India.

But in the old age of Runjeet a contractor for
the revenues of Esaukheyl was appointed over the
province, who, falsely alleging danger of rebellion
against the Sikh dynasty, sent a force to Esaukheyl
to make prisoner its reigning chief, Mohammed
Khan.

Mohammed escaped, with his second and ablest
son, Shah Niwaz. This youth took horse, and
scarcely rested by the way till he reached Peshawur,
when he threw himself at the feet of the Prince,
Runjeet Singh's grandson, to obtain justice for his
father.

His petition was heard, and Mohammed Khan
restored to his country. Years went by. Runjeet
Singh died; the Esaukheyl chief sent his son to offer
his renewed allegiance to his successor. As Shah
Niwaz returned he was seized by the agents of his
father's old enemy, and thrown into prison, where
he lay two and a-half years, and his father again
driven into flight.

At the end of the two and a-half years the Sikh
Government ordered Shah Niwaz to be sent to
Lahore; and the prime minister, Rajah Dhyan Singh,
was on the point of restoring him with his father
to Esaukheyl, when the vizier and the reigning
monarch were both murdered on the same day, and
the unhappy chief of Esaukheyl was again left in

hopeless exile. Their enemy died, but his son succeeded to his power and malice; and in 1847, when Lieutenant Edwardes first went into Bunnoo, he found Mohammed Khan, the rightful and loyal lord of the province, decrepit with old age and misfortune, and living in squalid dependence on a hospitable rebel.

" I heard the tale, and asked Dewan Dowlut Raie if it was true—if he had really got no order from the Crown to depose a subject chief and appropriate his lands? He admitted it was true, and he had none ; but in his judgment and conscience, it was necessary for the peace of the country, etc.

In the judgment and conscience of Sir Henry Lawrence, it was necessary for the peace of the country, and the honour of the British administration of Punjāb affairs, that such a Governor should be Governor no more ; so Dewan Dowlut Raie was superseded by General Van Cortlandt, and the old chief of Esaukheyl returned to his country and his rights—I trust, with all my heart, for ever.

In the sequel, it will be seen how his son, Shah Niwaz, joined my standard in the Mooltan war, and paid the debt of gratitude at the cannon's mouth. He was a faithful servant ; and may the prosperity of his family, under British rule, be the enduring monument over his grave ! "

# CHAPTER III.

DERA FUTTEH KHAN is the central town of the Dérajât, conveniently situated on the bank of one of the branches of the Indus. It contains thirty Hindū and sixteen Mohammedan shops. The original town is said to have been of great size, and stood far to the eastward of the present one. It was swept away by the Indus, and a second built more inland. This shared the same fate, and consequently the third and present colony is inferior in size and wealth to either of its predecessors.

The Sikhs did not call the surrounding district after the chief town, but Giràng, after the fort of that name, a few miles to the north of Dera Futteh Khan, and three or four from the bank of the Indus. It is a strong fort for that part of the world; and Runjeet Singh, who was no bad judge,

---

* I intended this interjectional passage to be given only in a note: but find it too interesting and valuable to be printed small; and though brief. the matter of it is more than enough for a chapter, being 'the history of the Punjāb in a nutshell.'

attached so much importance to it, that he never
consigned it to the charge of the Nazim of the
province, but kept it quite independent of his
authority, in the keeping of a true Sikh, named
Bhowanee Singh, and a garrison of seventy-one men,
whose pay amounted to six thousand and ninety
rupees a-year.

I call him a true Sikh, not more on account
of his incorruptible fidelity to Runjeet and his
descendants, than for his predatory instincts. The
very type and embodiment of the species Sikh,
*genus homo,* is a highwayman in possession of a
castle. Take any man of that nation—I care not
who—and give him a mud tower as his earthly
portion, and next week he will be like Ali Baba,
the Captain of Forty Thieves. Let him alone—
that is, don't overmatch him with kings and other
great policemen—and he will die a great man. It
is the history of the Punjāb in a nutshell.

Bhowanee Singh, who has led me into this philosophical digression, had all the elements of a great
rascal. He was small in stature, but his heart was
a large and a hard one, and its pulsations were
those of a sledge-hammer among the people round
him. It was impossible to look at his wild elfin
locks, and fiery eye, without clenching your fist—
he looked such a villain. Perched upon the battle-

ment of Giràng, he took an admirably just view of
his position.    He saw beneath him a plain very
often fertile, if very often barren, and in possession
of a people who were too great thieves themselves
not to submit to plunder as a law of the universe.
Beyond them was a plain still wilder, where rich
merchants fed their camels.    Nothing could be
easier than to ride out and take them.    The means
at his disposal were ample.    There was a strong
fort to sally out from, and come back to, and lock
up plunder ; and there was a garrison of seventy-
one soldiers, who had no objection, of course, to
be seventy-one thieves ; and who, moreover, would
cost nothing, but be paid by Government.    If the
victims complained to the Nazim of the province,
what cared he for the Nazim ?    Was he not particularly told to keep himself independent ?    And
if they carried their complaints to Lahore, he had
only to send a share of the plunder to Lahore also.
In short, Bhowanee Singh saw that there was a fine
opening.

Acting upon these views, he soon turned the
royal fort of Giràng into a nest of highway robbers ; the very people of the country were in his
pay and service ; and he extended his operations
like a net over the whole country between the
Indus and the Ooshteraunce hills, the boundary of

Sungurh and the boundary of Choudwan.   Herds
and herds of camels he caused the Beloochees to
drive away; and then sallying out with his horsemen, he pretended to pursue them, fired blank
cartridge till all the country echoed, routed his
own thieves, brought the rescued camels to Girâng,
and then claimed the gratitude of the owners, with
a heavy ransom equal to a quarter of the value.

And from all this there was no appeal found in
the Punjâb; and Bhowanee Singh went on thus for
I believe twenty years, doing evil, and growing rich.
At last the British came; and at this point Bhowanee Singh would have left off, if he had been the
really clever fellow that he had hitherto appeared.
But this is the way with bad men : they are certain
to break down.   Like ill-cast bells, they crack
when they are hard rung.   "What is the British
Resident to me?" said Bhowanee Singh : and he
robbed on.   Among others, one day his gang
pounced upon a herd of camels that belonged to
a Meankheyl merchant, whose name (I write from
memory) was, I think, Juhan Khan.   The Meankheyls, encamped hard by, took horse and pursued
the robbers, who, finding themselves pressed, divided,
and took separate paths across the jungle.   One
party was overtaken, and the furious Meankheyls
came down on them sword in hand.   Far in front

rode one on a foaming mare, and already he was
within a few yards of the spoilers, when the hinder
robber turned, stuck the butt of his spear into the
ground, and dropping on his right knee behind it,
planted his left foot firmly against the butt, while
with both hands he depressed the point, and
received the charge of the Meankheyl. Vainly
the horseman tried to turn it with his sword ; the
force of his own onset lent it strength, and entering his lungs, it issued at his back, and bore him
to the earth. It was Juhan Khan, and he died
two days after. The rest of the pursuers stayed to
pick up their leader, and the robbers made good
their retreat within the gates of the fort of Giràng.

Juhan Khan's surviving brother, Deen Mohammed, swore revenge; and betook himself to Mooltan,
where he heard there was a British officer. There
he found Lieutenant Nicholson, one of the Resident's assistants, who read his petition ; and writing
an English note on the back, told him to take it
on to me in Bunnoo, and he would get redress. I
sent for Bhowanee Singh, who swore he had seized
the camels because Juhan Khan would not pay his
trinnee, or tax on grazing. Deen Mohammed produced the Government receipt for the trinnee, and
the Governor of the province deposed that, had any
trinnee been due, Bhowanee Singh had nothing to

do with its collection ; so I made Bhowanee Singh deposit one hundred rupees for every camel, and the case stood over for trial, as the season for the return of the Powinduh caravans was expiring, and Deen Mohammed could stay no longer.    Meanwhile Bhowanee Singh was removed from his castle at Girâng, and brought a prisoner to Lahore, where he found for once that bribery was of no use.

It was not till my present visit to the very scene of the murder, that the trial of Bhowanee Singh came on.    His noble friends in the Lahore Durbar sent him honourably down, without fetter or handcuff, and an escort, more than a guard, of cavalry. I put him in irons.    Then, for the first time, the people of the country saw that his day was gone. A perfect " cloud of witnesses " rose up against the fallen robber ; and when at last, after a most laborious trial, Bhowanee Singh was convicted, and in consideration of the lax laws under which he had lived, was sentenced to only twelve years' imprisonment, and forfeiture of the deposit money to Deen Mohammed, the brother of the murdered Meankheyl was not the only one who thought the punishment a too " impotent conclusion " to a long career of rapine.

Reader, Bhowanee Singh was but one out of

hundreds of strong-handed oppressors of the Punjāb people, whom the British Resident and his
assistants tore up by the roots and flung into
the fire.  Our lives were made up of such interferences.

# CHAPTER IV.

## *THE MESSENGER.*

A S far as I have ever myself been able to form any conception of the principles observed by the British Government in the treatment of its officers, my impression has been that it always impedes the best men in their operations to the utmost of its ability ; and as soon as, in spite of all it can do, they have got accustomed to their duty and become entirely efficient in their position, sets them on different business in another place. I cannot find in Sir Herbert's diary any notice of the reasons for his leaving Bunnoo, or for General Taylor's coming there : but I suppose the substance of the matter to have been that at the time of the Sikh expedition there was no other British officer at hand of qualities known enough to be trusted with the delicate mission of its control, while yet the representation of British influence with the Sikh army did not in the least mean an appointment to the governorship of Bunnoo. Anyhow, having as it were swept and garnished the chamber of Bunnoo, and shaken up the cushions in the easy chair of its future occupant, we find him leaving the scene of these serviceable labours, to return no more, and at the time when the second main clause of this history begins, acting merely as a local magistrate in a small village on the eastern bank of the Indus.

From his diary in the second volume, I take what passages are necessary to my present purpose without inverted comma or interrupting space.

It was towards evening of April 22nd, 1848, at Dera Futteh Khan, on the Indus, that I was sitting in a tent full of Beloochee zumeendars, who were either robbers, robbed, or witnesses to the robberies of their neighbours, taking evidence in the trial of Bhowânee Singh, recounted in the last chapter.

Loud footsteps, as of some one running, were heard without,—came nearer as we all looked up and listened,—and at last stopped before the door. There was a whispering, a scraping off of shoes, and brushing off of dust from the wearer's feet, and then the curtain at the door was lifted, and a *kossid*, (running messenger,) stripped to the waist and streaming with heat, entered, and presented a letter-bag, whose crimson hue proclaimed the urgency of its contents. " It was

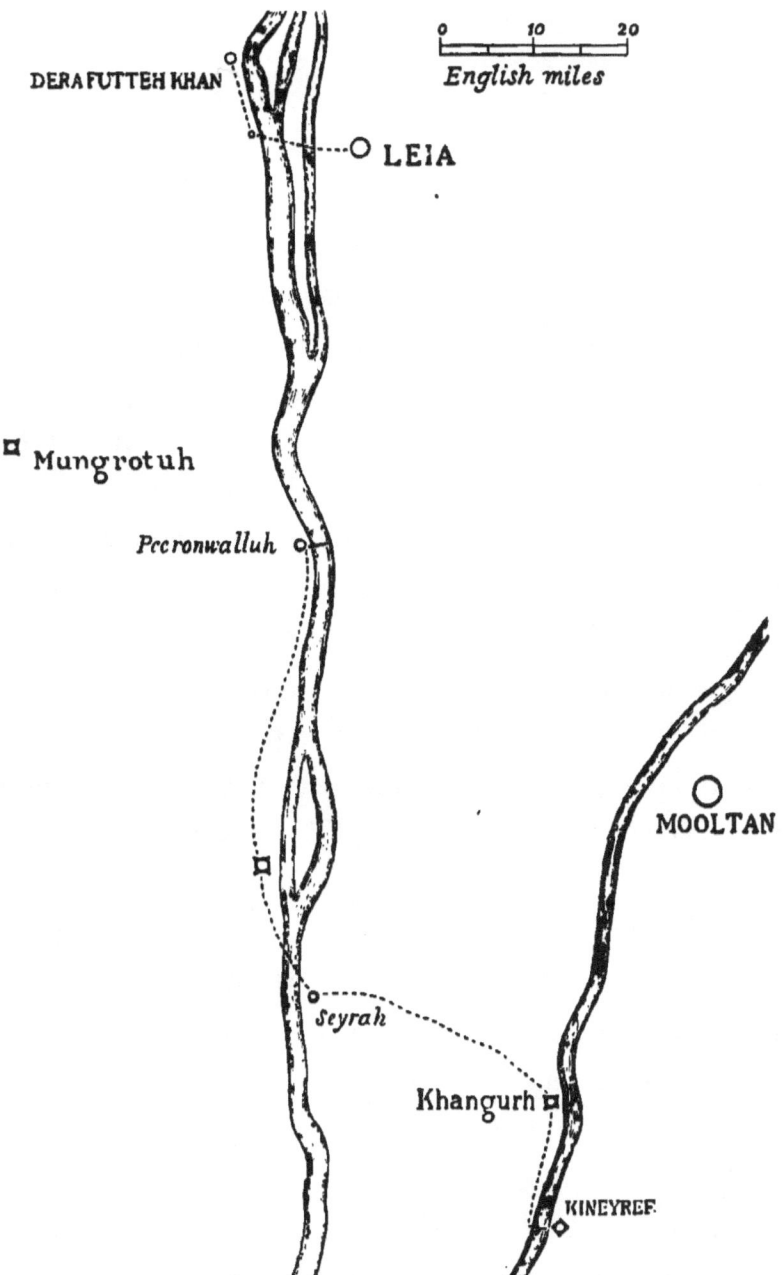

DERA FUTTEH KHAN

LEIA

English miles
0    10    20

Mungrotuh

Peeronwalluh

MOOLTAN

seyrah

Khangurh

KINEYREE

from the Sahib in Mooltan," he said, "to the Sahib in Bunnoo ; but, as I was here, I might as well look at it."

I took it up, and read the Persian superscription on the bag : "To General Cortlandt, in Bunnoo, or wherever else he may be." It was apparently not for me, but it was for an officer under my orders, and the messenger said it was on important public service ; I had, therefore, a right to open it if I thought it necessary. But there was something in the kossid's manner which alike *compelled* me to open it, and forbade me either to question him before the crowd around me, or show any anxiety about it.

So I opened it as deliberately as I could, and found an English letter enclosed, directed to either General Cortlandt or myself. It was a copy taken by a native clerk of a public letter addressed to Sir Frederick Currie by Mr. P. Vans Agnew, one of his assistants on duty at Mooltan, with a postscript in pencil written by Mr. Agnew, and addressed to us.

The following is a copy, and appended is a faithful fac-simile,* which will be regarded with mournful interest, as the last tracings of a hand ever generous, ever brave, which held fast honour and public duty to the death :

---

* I have reproduced here only the signature : see p. 146.

"Mooltan, 19th April, 1848.

"My dear Sir Frederick,

"You will be sorry to hear that, as Anderson and I were coming out of the fort gate, after having received charge of the fort by Dewan Moolraj, we were attacked by a couple of soldiers, who, taking us unawares, succeeded in wounding us both pretty sharply.

"Anderson is worst off, poor fellow. He has a severe wound on the thigh, another on the shoulder, one on the back of the neck, and one in the face.

"I think it most necessary that a doctor should be sent down, though I hope not to need him myself.

"I have a smart gash in the left shoulder, and another in the same arm. The whole Mooltan troops have mutinied, but we hope to get them round. They have turned our two companies out of the fort."

*Postscript in Pencil.*

"My dear Sir,

"You have been ordered to send one regiment here. Pray let it march instantly, or, if gone, hasten it to top-speed. If you can spare another, pray send it also. I am responsible for the measure. I am cut up a little, and on my back.

Lieutenant Anderson is much worse. He has five sword wounds. I have two in my left arm from warding sabre cuts, and a poke in the ribs with a spear. I don't think Moolraj has anything to do with it.* I was riding with him when we were attacked. He rode off, but is now said to be in the hands of the soldiery.

"Khan Singh and his people all right.

19th, 2 P.M.
To General Cortlandt, or
    Lieutenant Edwardes, Bunnoo."

During the perusal of the above letter, I felt that all eyes were on me, for no one spoke, not a pen moved, and there was that kind of hush which comes over an assembly under some indefinite

---

* This generous sentence is a complete answer to those who have supposed that Mr. Agnew drove Moolraj into rebellion by the harshness of his behaviour. Had anything passed between them to cause irritation, or give reasonable offence, Mr. Agnew would surely be the first to have remembered it. (H. E.)

feeling of alarm. I never remember in my life being more moved, or feeling more painfully the necessity of betraying no emotion. After lingering over the last few sentences as long as I could, I looked up at the kossid, and said : " Very good ! Sit down in that corner of the tent, and I'll attend to you as soon as I have done this trial." Then, turning to the gaping moonshees, I bade them " go on with the evidence," and the disappointed crowd once more bent their attention on the witnesses. But from that moment I heard no more. My eyes indeed were fixed mechanically upon the speakers, but my thoughts were at Mooltan, with my wounded countrymen, revolving how I ought to act to assist them.

In about an hour I had arranged the ways and means in my own mind, and that done, had no farther reason for concealment. I saw clearly what to do, and the sooner it was done the better.

So I broke up the court, and summoned an officer who was in charge of the ferry of the Indus between Dera Futteh Khan in my province, and Leia in Moolraj's ; and filled up the interval till he came by cross-questioning the kossid as to what he had seen himself. His account of the events themselves amounted to much the same as Mr.

Agnew had written ; but being a native of Mooltan, and better acquainted with the temper of Moolraj and his soldiery, he took a much less hopeful view of the position of the British officers, and believed that some guns, which he had heard since leaving Mooltan, announced the catastrophe which had in fact occurred.

Mooltan is about ninety miles (chiefly sand) from Dera Futteh Khan, and two broad rivers flow between them ; yet the kossid had accomplished the distance in exactly three days, after making several circuits to avoid provincial officials of Moolraj.

By the time the kossid had told his story, the officer I had sent for was announced. His name was Foujdar Khan, Alizye ; and as he took a distinguished part in the succeeding war, I claim the reader's attention to the singular chance which threw him in my way.

When Moolraj resigned the charge of the province of Mooltan, the collection of customs in his territory devolved upon the collector of the Lahore Government, who immediately wrote to his deputy at the Trans-Indus ferry to send a detachment of horsemen, under a sharp officer, across the river to Leia, to relieve the retiring customs' officer of Dewan Moolraj.

The deputy at Kuheeree selected Foujdar Khan for the duty; and he had been some days at the town of Leia when I arrived first at Dera Futteh Khan. As I was the chief authority in the province to which he belonged, Foujdar came across to pay his respects, or "make his salám," as the natives say, and I detained him several days. During this period I had only two interviews with him; but in discussing the subject of customs on the Indus, he impressed me so much with his extensive local knowledge, practical common sense, and singular power of mental calculation, that I could not but mark him down in my memory as a man who might be wanted on an occasion.

The occasion had now come; and the first man I summoned to my side, on the receipt of Mr. Agnew's call for assistance, was Foujdar Khan. Simultaneous intelligence of the outbreak had reached Leia also; and it is a singular coincidence that the letter which brought it to the Hakim or Governor of that town contained two orders: first, to seize all the boats at the Leia ferry, and prevent me from crossing the Indus; and secondly, to make Foujdar Khan (who was supposed to be still at Leia) a prisoner at all costs. Moolraj knew more of his ability at that time than I did;

but both he and I became still better acquainted with it afterwards.

My first question to Foujdar was, how many boats he could obtain for me by midnight? He immediately told me off on his fingers every ferry-boat within twenty or thirty miles; and horsemen were despatched in every direction to seize and bring them.

Meanwhile the whole camp was ordered to make instant preparations to cross the Indus.

With what purpose, what force, and in what firm acceptance of grave responsibility, this crossing of the Indus was ordered, the following extracts from the letters written on the instant, one to the Resident at Lahore, one to Mr. Vans Agnew, will explain.*

"To the Resident.    (April 22, 1848.)

"At 3 p.m. this day, an express from Mooltan, directed to General Cortlandt, reached my camp. I opened it, providentially, to see if it was on public business, and found a letter addressed to either General Cortlandt or myself, from Mr. Vans Agnew, communicating tidings of the dastardly

* I would fain have given both letters entire, but am obliged to sacrifice all details that confuse or delay the reader's clear conception of the course of events. (J. R.)

assault made on that gentleman and Lieutenant
Anderson at the gate of the fort of Mooltan, on
the 19th of April, particulars of which have ere
this reached you.

"Mr. Agnew called on General Cortlandt for
assistance ; and my duty to render it was plain.
I have accordingly resolved on making a forced
march to Mooltan, which is about sixty koss from
this, and hope by midnight sufficient boats will
have been collected from the neighbouring ferries
to allow the camp to cross the Indus.

"I have two guns, twenty zumbooruhs, twelve
infantry companies, and about three hundred and
fifty sowars : a small force, but quite strong
enough to create a diversion in favour of our two
countrymen, and whatever party the Maharajah
may still have in his city of Mooltan. I have
written to Mr. Vans Agnew to fall back on me,
if he is pressed, and rely on my speedy arrival.
From the desert nature of the road, and the
intense heat, I do not expect the men will be
able to make Mooltan before the 27th of April,
but every exertion shall be made.

"I feel sure that these measures will meet your
approbation. I wound up the revenue settlement
of this district two days ago ; and that of Dera
Ishmael Khan is of very secondary importance to

the duty of rescuing Mr. Vans Agnew and Lieutenant Anderson from their perilous situation."

To Mr. Vans Agnew I replied as follows:—

"Camp, Dera Futteh Khan,
April 22nd, 1848.

"My dear Agnew,

"Your letter of 19th April, to General Cortlandt, reached my camp at 3 p.m. this day; and I fortunately opened it to see if it was on public business.

"I need scarcely say that I have made arrangements for marching to your assistance at once.

"I have only a small force, but such as it is, you are welcome to it, and *me*.

"There are at this moment only three boats at the Ghât, and I have to collect others from the neighbouring ferries; but we shall manage, doubtless, to effect the passage in course of to-morrow, when the following route ought to bring us to Mooltan on 27th:—

> 23rd, left bank of Indus.
> 24th, Leia.
> 25th, Wells, half-way to Wander.
> 26th, Wander.
> 27th, Mooltan.

"Rely on it, it shall not be my fault if we are

a day later; but the very sound of our approach will be a check to your rascally enemies, and to *you*, as refreshing as the breeze which heralds the rising sun at morning. If you are pressed, pray bring away Anderson, and join me. With all my heart I hope you are both safe at this moment!

"I have written on to Bunnoo for Soobhan Khan's regiment, and a troop of horse artillery.

"Write, write, write! and with the sincerest wishes, believe me, in weal or woe,

"Yours, aye,

"HERBERT EDWARDES."

Alas! this letter was never destined to meet the eyes of either Agnew or Anderson. Those eyes were already closed; those hearts were still. The kossid who took it, heard the tidings of their death upon the road, and brought it back. I keep it still, among other sad memorials of those days.

To Lieutenant Taylor, who was with General Cortlandt in Bunnoo, I wrote the pith of the above two letters, and begged him to send a regiment of infantry and four guns, "sharp"; but on no account any other troops; for I felt certain, though I had never seen Mooltan, that if there was to be a war, and that fortress was to be reduced, the emergency must be met from Lahore. I went myself, not so much to fight Moolraj as to help my countrymen.

I am aware that it has been said, (and strangely enough, by many who desired nothing so much as a like opportunity of being useful; and who, had it fallen to their lot, would, I gladly believe, have used it honourably,) that I interfered where I had no call of duty, and levied soldiers to carry on a war for my own ambitious ends.

Perfectly satisfied with the approbation of my sovereign, country, the Indian and British Governments, and both Houses of Parliament, I could well afford to be silent; but having now printed, in extenso, poor Agnew's appeal for help, as an essential part of this narrative, I will just make two remarks upon it in passing;— that those I allude to may in charity be supposed to have been ignorant of its existence: but if not, I should have deserved even their contempt, had I been coward enough to disregard it.

As soon as ever the troops who were with me at Dera Futteh Khan were ready, the march was commenced without delay. In describing the town of Dera Futteh Khan, I mentioned that it was situated on a branch of the Indus.

We had, consequently, to cross this branch, or 'nullah,' and an island three miles wide on the other side, before we could reach the main stream of the Indus.

On this nullah there was only one boat; and no others were brought round, because we wanted them more on the Indus itself, where by midnight on the 22nd of April we had only collected three. It may easily be conceived, therefore, what a tedious operation it was to ferry over twelve hundred soldiers, with guns, camel-swivels, horses, carts, and camp-followers, in one punt which would only hold forty or fifty men at a time. All night, after the moon rose, the men were hard at it; and though the punt foundered and went down towards morning, and obliged the Sikh regiment to ford up to their chins, with their arms and accoutrements in a bundle on their heads, the men behaved most cheerfully; and by noon of the 23rd, horse and foot had all reached the Indus.

There we found that no fresh boats had arrived from the neighbouring Gháts; and the horsemen who had been sent to the nearest, returned with the tidings that Moolraj's Kárdárs had secured all the boats on the left bank, and issued orders to the ferrymen to cross no troops.

So we were obliged to begin the passage of the Indus with three boats. It is a grand river at all seasons, but at this it was mighty and terrible. Each trip of the boats was a little voyage, and occupied between two and three hours.* But there was no help for it, and we sat down on the margin to watch the tedious process, and speculate on what was before us.

Ensconced in a palanquin I had borrowed at Koláchee (for the wound in my knee which I got in the Nássur skirmish, on the 16th of March, was still so bad that I could neither ride nor walk), I lay on the bank impatiently expecting the arrival of more boats. No tents were allowed to be pitched, not even my own, so as to be ready whenever boats arrived ; and as everything was packed up, we got nothing to eat all day. At night a luxurious little gentleman named Hookum Chund, of the Lahore Secretariat, who could not possibly forego his curry, brought me half his dinner with the true compassion of an epicure ; but I was more fit to be eaten myself after the broiling sun of a long April day.

At sunset a storm sprang up, and still farther embarrassed our slow passage ; and I had given

* Width of stream not told, nor rate of current ! The river was in flood, and on the map (p. 143) is three miles wide, opposite Leia, between its unflooded banks.

up all hopes of crossing the Indus that night,
and had fallen asleep in the pálkee, when loud
shouts proclaimed the arrival of thirteen boats
from Kuheeree, a ferry about twenty-five miles
higher up the river, where Foujdar's horsemen had
arrived just in time to prevent Moolraj's people
from carrying them off.

The moon rose about the same moment, as
if bidding us be diligent, and the storm lulled ;
so packing all the boats full of soldiers, I put
myself like an Admiral in the van, and led the
fleet across.

A melancholy accident occurred in the passage.
One of the boats was very old and rickety, and
before it could make the left bank, filled with
water and went down. It was first reported to
me that out of eighty souls, only nine or ten
had escaped ; but it subsequently appeared that
out of about fifty, only eight were lost. The
stern of the boat found the bottom, and the
prow remaining in the air, enabled almost all to
save themselves.

Before midnight the passage seems to have been
secured, and Edwardes, on the left bank of the
Indus, lies down for a soldier's swift sleep. Before
the dawn of the early April morning he is waked
by Foujdar Khan with the news from a horseman.

of Tâk that Agnew and Anderson are both dead,
and Moolraj in open revolt. (Particulars here
omitted—they are too sorrowful. I pass them
over with the comment only, that while the
absolute force of the British army consists in the
resolution of its officers never to shrink from an
imperative task, whatever the inadequacy of their
means, its failures and the severity of its tasks are
always traceable, either to the want of foresight
and sense in the home government, or, as in this
instance, to the impatience of officers too confident
in national prestige, and too much like schoolboys
in provoking fortune.)

That very morning, April 25th, (resuming now
Sir Herbert's diary,) before getting out of my
bed, I dictated, signed, and dispatched twenty
orders : eight to officers at important posts
in General Cortlandt's province behind me, to
warn them of what had occurred, and bid them
be on the alert and steadfast, but not alarmed ;
eight others to Kárdárs and other district officers of
Moolraj's Cis- and Trans-Indus in the country round
me, transferring them to the Maharajah's service, if
they were loyally disposed, and bidding them tran-
quillise the minds of the people ; two to detached
officers to join me with their men ; and two only
to enlist new ones. For I had no intention of initi-

ating hostilities against an enemy like Moolraj, in possession of a fortress like Mooltan ; and I was not yet awakened to the necessity of either creating a faithful party in my own camp, or enlisting the soldiers of the country, to prevent them from being enlisted by Moolraj. The latter I soon found to be imperative.

All our people being over the Indus on the night of the 24th, I marched to Leia on the morning of the 25th, and encamped south-east of the city, of which we took peaceful possession, Moolraj's Governor, Ruttun Chund, having retired with his men at our approach. The rest of the officials had remained, in compliance with my orders, and came out with the chief people of the city to receive us. They all brought very long faces, and very short presents.*

Leia is a very extensive city, built of burnt brick, with numerous wells around its suburbs. It is the chief town of the southern Sindh Sâgur Doâb, and, at the time I speak of, was a great commercial dépôt for the Cabul merchants. It was consequently an important place, and I at once put an officer in

---

* In the East, an inferior never approaches a superior with an empty hand ; and though European masters only touch the offered present as an acknowledgment of the compliment, yet officials keep up the ceremony, and neglecting it is a mark of disrespect. The amount offered increases with the rank and loyalty of the offerer.

charge of it for the Maharajah, and told him to collect the revenue as fast as he could.

Having done this, I wrote to Sir Frederick Currie, as follows :

"LIEUTENANT EDWARDES TO THE RESIDENT AT LAHORE.

"Camp, Leia, Cis-Indus,
"April 25th, 1848.

"I reached this place this morning, and have encamped south-east of the city, covering it from Mooltan.

"You have, I hope, already got my letters advising you of my determination to cross the Indus as soon as I heard of the attack on Agnew and Anderson, and move on Mooltan in the hope of saving them. That hope is declared by general rumour to be hope no more. Agnew and Anderson are said to be both dead, killed by their own men ; Khan Singh a prisoner, and Dewan Moolraj going all lengths in preparations to maintain himself in the fort.

"This I fully believe, as this Doâb is full of his emissaries raising soldiers ; and had I been a day later, I could not have crossed the Indus, instructions having been sent to the Kárdár of Leia, to seize the boats, raise three thousand men, and hold the place.

" My crossing took him by surprise, and he fled, with the Leia Thánnah, to Mooltan.

" Agnew and Anderson dead, and the Sirdar's force either traitors or prisoners in Mooltan, I have no object in advancing further. Neither could I cross the Chenab, if I wished. Neither would it be prudent to wish it, if I could."

## CHAPTER V.

### *ON GUARD AT LEIA.*

THE conclusion of Lieutenant Edwardes' letter
to the Resident, partly quoted in the preceding chapter, introduces a new phase in his
position, thus :*—

"Leia is an important city, and the capital of
this Doâb. Its mere possession by the Sirkar's
troops flies through the country, and inflicts a
blow on Moolraj's prestige, and prevents hundreds
of mercenaries from joining his standard. Of this
I have hourly proof. Still my position, I cannot
but see, is one of great uncertainty and peril.
If Moolraj has the spirit and skill to throw a
force with guns over the Chenab at once, he
might crush us, and return in a canter to Mooltan
before our own troops can come from Lahore.
Already, he is said to have done so (crossed the
Chenab). I believe the truth to be that he in-

---

* I keep the inverted commas, to distinguish the letter to the
Resident from Lieut. Edwardes' diary.

tends to do so. Perhaps, ere this his force has crossed.

"My mind is made up. I shall throw up intrenchments here and stand. Great ends will be secured by my success; immense confusion follow a retreat.

"I am entertaining men, for the double purpose of securing them from joining Moolraj, and holding this Doâb against the rebels. The Doâb swarms with mercenary swordsmen, ever ripe for mischief. The regiment and four guns, which I have summoned from Bunnoo, cannot reach here till the 7th or 8th of May, and the interval will be one of immense anxiety.

"I calculate that you will have sent off our field brigade on the 24th of April, and that it will reach Mooltan in ten days'; but trust that it will only be the vanguard of a regular army, for the reduction of Mooltan will be no child's play. I know not if you have good information from Mooltan, therefore I may as well state my views of this affair.

"I think Moolraj has been involved in rebellion against his will, and, being a weak man, is now persuaded by his officers that there is no hope for him but in going all lengths; that the origin of the rebellion was the natural dislike of the

Puthàns, Beloochees, and Mooltances (men of high family, courage, and false pride) to be turned adrift, after a life spent in military service well rewarded ; and that these men will fight desperately, and die hard, unless a provision is held out to them just before the siege (before the last moment they would not accept it, and only then will they do so with dexterous *vikálut* [diplomacy], carried on by one of their own blood, who knows their points of honour).

"If I might, without offence, offer a military suggestion, when you have such able soldiers in Lahore, it would be that Bháwul Khan be called on to cross the Sutlej instanter, and co-operate with a British force from Lahore and a brigade from Sindh.

"Bháwul Khan's country also is full of these noble Beloochees and Mooltances ; and already Moolraj has summoned them to join his standard, and they will come if not detained by Bháwul Khan.

"I have opened a correspondence with Moolraj, more with the object of getting a kossid unobstructed into Mooltan, than with any hope of persuading the Dewan to follow my advice, and throw himself on your mercy before things go any further.

"This letter goes by a kossid, *viâ* Jhung, by

which route please send me instructions as soon
as you can, and let me know, daily, what movements are made on Mooltan, that I may co-
operate in any way in my power.

"There are two guns and four or five hundred
men at Jhung, who would be very welcome here.
At present, I am very much like a Scotch terrier
barking at a tiger. If a week only passes over, I
shall have got together enough men to hold on.
If not, we are in God's hands, and could not be
better placed."

Determined now to seize as much of the rebel
Dewan's country as I could, I wrote this day to
Ali Khan, of Koláchee, to join me as rapidly as
he could, with one hundred horse and two
hundred foot of the tribe of Gundapoor ; to
Ubdoolla Khan, chief of the Óoshteraunees, who
but a few days before was in rebellion himself,
to send me one hundred of his best mountain
marksmen ; Hôt Khan, of same tribe, to bring
another hundred ; Ubeezur Khan, of Koondee, in
Tâk, to bring twenty horsemen from his native
village ; and lastly, to Foujdar Khan, Alizye,
whom I daily found more useful, I gave the
comprehensive order to enlist every soldier of the
Sindh Sâgur Doâb who was still out of employ,
and preferred the royal standard to the rebel's.

Next day I wrote to the Resident as follows :—

"LIEUT. EDWARDES TO THE RESIDENT AT LAHORE.

"Camp. Leia, April 26th, 1848.

"Common report still declares that Moolraj has thrown a force, with guns, across the Chenab, to oppose my advance ; but my own spies have not yet had time to return, and the latest trustworthy intelligence contradicts the report above mentioned, and says that the greatest consternation reigns in Mooltan, where the garrison (officers and all) are engaged in cutting the ripe corn and carrying it into the fort. They are very hard up also for grass. In this condition, it is not probable that the Dewan will detach men and guns, and weaken his own position. I am entertaining men in self-defence, and to check the tide of recruiting which was flowing to Mooltan. Moolraj is enlisting, right and left, and has unlimited command of money.

"I cannot convey to you any idea of the happy effect of our crossing the Indus, and occupying the great body of Moolraj's country ; but I may say that it has arrested an extensive rebellion, and made the difference between a siege and a campaign.

"I have thought it best to tell Kishen Lal, the Jhung Adawlutee, to send me his two guns and four hundred men forthwith.

"A Puthán gave me a good account to-day of the Mooltan outbreak, and it seems that the Sikh troops behaved most shamefully, going over without any reason whatever. Agnew died like a hero, disdaining to fly and refusing to yield. His head was cut off by Moolraj's soldiers.

"Unanimity is far from existing in the rebel garrison. Three of Moolraj's principal officers (Surbulund Khan, Badozye, and his son, Sadik Mohammed Khan, and Gholám Moostapha Khan, Khághwánee), were so opposed to the whole proceeding, that they refused to set their seals to the Koran, leaving themselves open to conviction.

"I hope soon to hear of the advance of our British troops from Lahore, and may take this opportunity of expressing my conviction, that to send any other troops (i.e. Sikh) to Mooltan, after what has occurred, would be to run the most imminent risk of a treacherous catastrophe."

In the evening of April 26th, I ordered the colonel of the Sikh regiment to look quietly about for a position to intrench, on the Mooltan side of Leia, for I expected before night to hear that Moolraj had thrown troops across the Chenab,— in which event, relying on the fidelity of the Sikh troops that were with me, it was my intention to have made a stand at Leia.

On the 27th I received trustworthy intelligence that Moolraj's Kárdár at Dera Ghazee Khan, Longa Mull by name, had received " the fiery cross " from his master, and was going all lengths in stirring up the country trans-Indus to rebellion. As this would carry the war into General Cortlandt's province of Dera Ishmael Khan, I instantly took measures for its defence by summoning the General, with another regiment, two more guns, and one hundred horse, from Bunnoo to Girâng, there to co-operate with me as circumstances might require. The same train of thought made me consider well Lieutenant Taylor's position in Bunnoo, when his force should be thus weakened ; and I advised his calling for another regiment from Peshawur, while I did what I could to secure the peace of the country around him, by desiring General Cortlandt to bring away with him (nominally as recruits, but in reality hostages), as many sons and brothers of the chiefs of Bunnoo and Murwut as he could enlist.

In the course of this day two very different communications reached me from Mooltan. One from a Nâssur merchant, named Sâdoollah Khan, who related how the murdered British officers had been indebted to the Afghan merchants at Mooltan for burial ; that they had covered the bodies with silk scarfs, and carried them to the grave in rude imitation of the British funerals they had seen. As the only return in my power, I immediately released two men of the Nàssur tribe, who had been sentenced to six months' imprisonment for plundering; nor did I regret this acknowledgment when subsequent inquiry proved that the Cabul merchants had only reproached Moolraj with not giving an honourable burial to men who were not even his enemies.

The other communication was as follows :—

"THE MOOLTAN SIKHS TO THE TROOPS UNDER
"LIEUTENANT EDWARDES.

"April 22nd, 1848.

"By the favour of the Holy Gooroo.*

"Now we, in accordance with the Gooroo's command, have written to all of you, our Khalsa brethren. Those of you who are true and sincere Sikhs, will come to us here. You will receive plenty of pay, and the approbation of the Dewan.

"The Maharajah Duleep Singh will, by the Gooroo's grace, be firmly established in his kingdom; there will be no more cow-killing, and our holy religion will prosper.

"All believing Sikhs, who trust in the Gooroo,

* I give only the close, which is the essential part, of this document, which at its opening gives a painful recapitulation of the circumstances of the death of the two British officers. The Gooroo is the High Priest of the Sikhs. See note by Lady Edwardes at end of Chapter VI.

will place confidence in our words, and, joining us, will honour his name.

" Forward copies of this manifesto to all our Sikh brethren, and delay not ; for those who spread this intelligence will meet with the approbation of the Gooroo.

" You know that all are mortal ; whoever, therefore, as becomes a sincerely believing Sikh, devotes his life to the service of the Gooroo, will obtain fame and reputation in *this world*.

" The Maharajah and his mother are in sorrow and affliction. By engaging in their cause, you will obtain their favour and support. Gird up your loins under the protection of the Gooroo, and Govind Singh will preserve his sanctity. Make much of a few words."

The circumstances under which this plain-spoken document reached my hands, and the reflections it excited in my mind, were thus reported to the Resident.

"Camp, Leia, April 27th, 1848.

" A most important document has fallen into my hands, being a solemn summons, in the name of all that is holy in the Khalsa religion, from the Sikh soldiers in the fort of Mooltan to the regiment of Sikhs along with me, to march immediately and join the rebels in Mooltan.

"It is signed and sealed by all the officers who went from Lahore with Agnew; but along with it they have brought me a counterbond of fidelity, signed by all the officers of the Futteh Pultun,* professedly drawn up in ignorance of the Mooltan document, and suggested only by the crisis in which we are placed.

"If this paper (with the invitation from Mooltan) has not been seen by the whole regiment, how long will it be before another paper comes? and will that also fall into my hands? Depend upon it, the paper which I have got is a circular, and it is right to be prepared for the possible consequences of its favourable reception among the Sikh soldiers at all points.

"Doubtless you have made up your mind that a British force must go to Mooltan, and this will naturally bring in fresh reinforcements from the rear.

"I do not send the paper to you, as it is too valuable to be risked in the *dâk* (Post-office) at this time.

"How strangely now do Lawrence's arguments return to my mind, for banishing that Jezebel † from

---

* The Sikh regiment now under Lieutenant Edwardes' command at Leia.

† Who? Moolraj's mother?

the Punjâb ! she is a leaven of evil, which some day
will leaven a fearful lump of political trouble. You
have not forgotten, I dare say, her sending a slave-
girl on a secret embassy to Mooltan, last June or
July, and her impudent excuse, that she wanted a
white âk tree for enchantments. The " tree " has
now put forth its leaves, and their *rung* (colour,
species) is much what might have been expected.

"With the above exception, all is going on well!
Our presence has, at a stroke, secured quiet in this
Doâb, and those who are disaffected can only sneak
off to Mooltan. I have most fortunately got with
me an exceedingly clever Puthán, of good family,
named Foujdar Khan, who is related to many of
Moolraj's chief officers, and knows every mercenary
on both sides of the Indus. This has enabled me
to summon some twenty or thirty leaders, whose
swords are in the market ; and in a few days I
shall have a levy of about three thousand Putháns
and Beloochees, equal to twice their number of
Sikhs, for any work along the banks of the
Attock."

I could have little doubt in my own mind that
the paper addressed by the Mooltan Sikhs to the
troops under me—which had been received by a
Sikh officer in those troops from his own uncle,
who was a rebel in Mooltan, and had been kept by

him a whole night, and half the next day in camp, before bringing it to me—must have been seen and read by every Sikh soldier in my force. And if seen and read, then assuredly had it gone straight to the heart of every reader, for it breathed the very essence of Sikh feeling, and faithfully interpreted the aspirations of the nation. The seeds therefore had been sown, and the harvest was for me to reap.

But I knew that it could neither spring, nor ripen, without the sunshine of opportunity, and the golden showers of Moolraj's gold. It was my duty to see that it got neither ; and above all, to take care that no exhibition of distrust on my part precipitated the troops into disaffection.

In reply, therefore, to the bond of fidelity, which the colonel and officers of the Sikh regiment had volunteered, I assured them that I should have great pleasure in forwarding it to their Sovereign at Lahore, who would doubtless be pleased with their attachment at a moment when a provincial Governor had displayed such ingratitude towards the nation which had raised his family from insignificance. But I warned them, nevertheless, to watch over the honour of their regiment. I told them " that the rebels in Mooltan had conspired to involve my troops in the certain ruin which awaited themselves; that they would send traitors to corrupt the soldiers in this camp; and as all were not wise and experienced, it became the officers to be vigilant, to seize any such messengers, turn them out of their lines, and save their regiment from disgrace."

That very day a Sikh spy from Mooltan was found in camp, and brought to me, like the paper, after all the mischief had been done. Finding that he had been long enough in camp to deliver as many letters and messages as he liked, I pretended to be quite satisfied with his account of himself, and showed no suspicion.

But my confidence in the Sikh soldiers of the camp was gone; and I felt assured that the march of a British army from Lahore was the only event which could secure even their neutrality.

This was not my opinion only. In the dusk of the evening, while I was eating my dinner, the adjutant of the Artillery, a man of Hindūstan, begged to be allowed to speak to me, and when admitted, besought me on his knees, and in considerable agitation, to move his guns to the right, with a company of Poorbeeuhs on each side, as he had every reason to believe that the Sikh regiment was conspiring mischief, and where the guns were then, they might be seized at any time.

He added, "They have a prophecy, that in two years and a half from their defeat on the Sutlej, their independence shall be restored. That time has exactly come!"

Still later at night, when the old grey-headed adjutant of the Poorbeeuh Infantry came to report that he had visited all the guards and sentries, he threw himself at my feet, and with tears in his eyes implored me to be on my guard, for he had served many, many years in the service of the Sikhs, and seen all their revolutions; and if the Futteh Pultun was not brewing mischief now, he (Sirdar Singh) knew nothing about their character.

"Nonsense!" I said; "what do you judge by?" He replied: "By their letting none but Sikhs come into their lines these last two days, and going in and out of each other's tents in knots, and holding meetings, and an unusual kind of swaggering air with them, such as the Sikh soldiers used to have at Lahore before the Sutlej war, when they had the government in their hands, and were buying and selling their own chiefs!"

The impressive and earnest manner of these two faithful men had a great effect upon me. Their experience set the seal to my own observations and suspicions, and I felt at once all the horror of being betrayed, and the revolting necessity of wearing the mask of confidence.

Before going to bed I wrote to my friend Taylor, and telling him my own position, warned him to be on his guard against the troops in Bunnoo.

Next day I wrote again to the Resident.

"Camp, Leia, April 29th, 1848.

"I have no longer any doubt of there being a mutinous correspondence going on between the Mooltan traitors (Khan Singh's troops) and the Sikhs in my camp ; and it must be sufficiently evident, for the adjutant of the two guns along with me came to me last night, and, on his knees, begged me to put the guns on the right, and away from the Sikhs, who he said were conspiring among themselves secretly in the lines. I cannot, of course, move the guns without declaring my suspicions ; and see nothing for it but to be firm, patient, and vigilant, hastening the recruiting of Puthans, and awaiting the arrival of Cortlandt with Sobhan Khan's regiment, which I believe is trustworthy.

"But he cannot reach till the 6th, so that I have a whole week of this anxiety to endure.

"Not the least difficult task is that of meeting,

with cordiality and politeness, the Colonel of the Futteh Pultun and his officers, and Bhaee Ameera Buksh, knowing all the time that they have marked me for their prey.

" I have replied, however, to the bond of fidelity, which they volunteered to send me, in such terms as to appeal at once to their loyalty and cupidity ; and I send you the originals herewith, thinking it would be a good thing if you were to make a great fuss in the Durbar, about the bright example thus set by the Futteh Pultun ; send them an ell-long purwánna of approval, and, by assuming them to have virtue, induce them still to wear its mask.

" It is probable that the Sikhs, whatever their designs are, will not disclose them till the last moment, reserving themselves for a *grand coup* in front of Mooltan. I shall wait here, there-fore, until joined by Cortlandt, by which time I hope to have got three thousand Puthàns together, and thus be too strong for the Sikhs in my own camp. I propose then to move forwards, and throw myself into a small fort named Moondeh, twenty-five koss from this place, and about fifteen from Mooltan, pitching the Sikhs and majority of the camp outside, taking the guns inside. In that attitude I should be prepared for friend or foe, which seem just now synonymous terms.

"It is indeed mortifying to know that the only obstacles in my way are the royal troops. If I had not a Sikh soldier in the camp, my mind would be at rest.

"Accounts from Mooltan describe the garrison as constantly engaged in laying in stores, and preparing for resistance."

On the 29th I redoubled my former efforts to enlist Puthàns ; and at the close of an anxious day received the startling intelligence contained in the annexed letter :

> "Camp, Moorawallah, on the left bank of the Indus,
> opposite Dera Futteh Khan, May 1st, 1848.

"I have now to inform you that, late on the evening of the 29th, one of my own kossids returned from Mooltan, and brought the intelligence that Dewan Moolraj had at last made the move which, ever since my arrival in Leia, I had apprehended, and thrown eight heavy guns and between four and five thousand men across the Chenab, to oppose me, which force would reach Leia without fail on the 1st of May.

" Four courses were open to me :—

" 1. To intrench myself, either inside or outside the town of Leia, and fight it out.

" 2. To move east on Munkhera, the great central fort of the Desert.

" 3. To fall back on Bukkur, three marches to the north, and opposite to Dera Ishmael Khan, where there is a small fort, and await the arrival of General Cortlandt with reinforcements, expected at Dera on the 2nd of May.

" 4. To re-cross the Indus, and await General Cortlandt, under the fort of Girâng.

" Under any circumstances, the first plan would have been hazardous, for my whole force does not amount nearly to one thousand five hundred men, which are too few to hold the streets of a large town like Leia ; and my two horse artillery guns in an intrenchment outside would soon be silenced by eight heavy guns.    But doubting, as I did,.the loyalty of two-thirds of my men—nay, believing that they had themselves invited the hostile move-ment—I determined at all costs to avoid the double danger of a collision.

" Plans No. 2 and 3 I rejected for similar reasons.

" All these considerations led me to prefer making only one short march to the Indus, and awaiting General Cortlandt at Girâng on the other bank. The Killadar of Girâng is also a Puthán of my own appointment.

"Accordingly, yesterday morning we marched from Leia to this place, on the left bank of the Indus, and collected boats for embarkation; but I strictly forbade any one to cross, resolving to wait one more day on this side of the Indus, and see if anything might turn up in our favour.

"This morning another kossid has arrived from Mooltan, and says that, out of the four thousand five hundred men ordered to Leia, only five hundred have crossed the Chenab, and are encamped on the right bank.

"I now hope, therefore, to be able to hold my ground on this side of the Indus, until General Cortlandt can come up; when, if he has reliance on the Moossulmán regiments with him, and four guns, I shall lose no time in resuming my former position at Leia, so advantageous for the administration of the Doáb, and co-operation in any plans you may have formed for the reduction of Mooltan. Already I have sent a party of cavalry to Leia, to secure intelligence, collect customs, encourage friends, and show foes that we are not yet gone."

# CHAPTER VI.

## *EVENING GUNFIRE.*

### "LIEUTENANT EDWARDES TO THE RESIDENT AT LAHORE.

"Camp, Dera Futteh Khan Ghát,
"May 3rd, 1848.

"IT is with regret I inform you that I have been obliged to re-cross the Indus. On the 1st of May I reported to you that I had retired from Leia to the left bank of the river, but I hoped to be able to maintain my ground in the Sindh Ságur Doáb until General Cortlandt's arrival, as I had heard that the eight guns, and majority of the four thousand men, sent against us by Moolraj, had halted on the left bank of the Chenab.

"The halt appears to have been nothing more than the delay unavoidable in crossing troops and guns over a large river at this season of the year; and on the morning of the 2nd of May their advanced guard suddenly appeared at Kofilah, only four koss from Leia.

"It was, however, still doubtful whether the
guns had come on, or not ; and I again advanced
the whole of my cavalry to Leia, under Sirdar
Mohammed Khan and Foujdar Khan, to ascertain
the force of the rebels,—to surprise the Kofilah
party if it was unsupported by guns in the rear,
—and to cover our retreat, if it proved to be
only the advanced guard of the enemy's main
body.

"They had scarcely left camp, when they were
met by another kossid, with the information that
Moolraj's guns and main body were indeed
within eight koss of Leia, to the south ; but they
gallantly carried out their orders, reached Leia
in the evening, threw out sowars to Kofilah, and
having ascertained beyond all doubt the character
of the hostile movement, fell back in good order
at midnight.

"The intelligence brought by the kossid last
mentioned, decided me to lose no time ; and,
striking the tents at mid-day, I crossed the whole
baggage and cattle of the force to the right bank
of the Indus before nightfall, retaining only the
guns and infantry. The men, fully accoutred, lay
down in a half-moon, with the river in the rear,
and the empty boats drawn up ready for embarkation. In this order we awaited the return of the

cavalry, and day ; at dawn this morning the cavalry and guns crossed the Indus in two detachments, and about eight o'clock I brought up the rear with the infantry, just about the time when the enemy must have been marching into Leia, twelve miles behind us.

"I assure you that I gave up the Doâb with the greatest reluctance ; but I have already, in my last letter, fully given my last reasons for avoiding so unequal a collision as must have taken place, between two guns and fifteen hundred men, (of one thousand of whom the fidelity was very doubtful,) and eight guns and four thousand men, united in a desperate cause, and encouraged by the knowledge of having friends in my camp. The mortification of the retreat, and possibly its condemnation by those who know not the difficulties of my position, can only be personal to myself; whereas a defeat of the Sirkar's troops, in any quarter at the present moment, could not fail to have a disheartening influence on the army now advancing from Lahore, and seriously increase the difficulty of quelling the rebellion in Mooltan.

"As it is, my withdrawal from the Doâb can only be temporary. General Cortlandt, with another regiment (of Moossulmâns), and I believe six guns, will join me to-morrow, when we shall be in a condition to re-cross, and engage the rebels."

I shall not readily forget these events. To retreat at all, at any time, and under any circumstances, must be mortifying enough to a soldier. But the circumstances under which I had to retreat were these.

I was the only man in the whole camp who wanted to retreat!

The Sikh soldiers, who were the majority, had, there is every reason to believe, sold me. My very price had been agreed upon : twelve thousand rupees to the regiment for joining the rebels in the battle, and twelve thousand more if they brought over my head with them. It is needless, therefore to add, that with twenty-four thousand rupees to lose on one side, and merely honour on the other, the Futteh Pultun, to a man, was for standing fast at Leia. "What did I want to retreat for? Did I doubt their fidelity, or their courage? They would throw themselves into the town of Leia, erect barricades, and hold the place to all eternity. As for Moolraj's troops, though they were twenty to one, they should be eaten up! Only place implicit confidence in *them*, and I should never repent it!" (Which was probably true; for they would not have given me time.)

On the other hand, the faithful few, the artillery, the Poorbeeuh infantry, and the newly-raised Puthâns of the last week, were indignant at the bare notion of retreating; for it is a maxim of war among high-minded Asiatics, and especially Puthâns, that, " having advanced your right foot, it is honourable to bring the left up to it ; but to draw the right back to the left is a disgrace." But, I asked, " Suppose the enemy is obviously too strong for you ?" " Then stand and die ! " was the rash, but chivalrous response.

So there I stood alone among my soldiers ; some traitors, some true men, but all urging me to prove a fool, all fearing I might prove a coward.

I esteem it not the least of my little victories, that I stuck that day to my own opinion. There was not a shadow of doubt in my mind as to the course which ought to be pursued ; and I resolved accordingly to pursue it. For I again repeat a sentiment which I have before expressed in these volumes, that he who has to act upon his own responsibility is a slave if he does not act also on his own judgment.

Turning, therefore, to all the officers, false and true, I said : " It is my deliberate opinion that this force is incapable of resisting such an one as the rebels have sent against us, either in the open field, or in an intrenched position. To attempt it would be to sacrifice many lives in vain ; and I consider it, therefore, my duty to retreat. As to military maxims, every country has its own ; and among my countrymen (who are not considered very bad soldiers !) it is reckoned very bad generalship to fight unless there is a reasonable chance of victory. Let us therefore retreat, and reinforce ourselves. A long war is before us ; and the day will soon come when I shall call on you all to prove the valour of which you now make such display. We shall then see who is brave and who is not."

Next day the retreat was made, but with reluctance ; and the following colloquy between some Sikh soldiers of the rear-guard was over-heard by my own servants.

"What shall we do with this Sahib of ours ? "

"Oh ! kill him of course—what else ?"

"D'ye think so ? Well, I vote we *don't* kill him."

"What then ? You wouldn't let him off?"

"No !" (with concentrated malignity,) " I'd *make a Sikh of him !*"

"What for ?"

"Why, when he was a regular Sikh, and had taken the páhul,* I'd then make him carry bricks and mortar in a wicker basket on his head, as he made us do at Bunnoo, building that fort of Duleepgurh. I should just like to see how he'd like it."

And that night of May 2nd, when we lay down on the bank of the Indus, in a half-moon, with our backs to the river,—shall I ever forget it? There was a mutual distrust between the faithful and unfaithful parties of the soldiery. Not a word had been spoken, no duty refused, no symptom of open mutiny; and yet both sides knew each other, avoided each other, and were getting angry with each other. To make the best of it, I put the two guns in the centre, with the faithful Poorbeeuhs right and left, and lay down behind them. This secured the artillery, and divided the Sikh regiment into wings, right and left of the Poorbeeuhs. The new Puthán levies, and other horsemen, were thrown out as a picket to Leia.

Wearily and sleeplessly passed the night; the picket having ascertained the proximity of the

* The "páhul" is the initiation into the Sikh religion. and consists chiefly, I believe, of pledging attachment to its ordinances in a draught of water, which has been mystically stirred up with a sword or other weapon of steel or iron.

enemy, fell back from Leia ; and when morning dawned, there must be no delay in re-crossing to our own side of the Indus.

Then arose the question, who was to go over first ?    I found myself at the schoolboy puzzle of the Fox, the Geese, and the Ferryman.

If the faithless went over first, they would keep the boats on the other side, and leave the faithful to be cut up by the enemy ; if the faithful went over first, the faithless might join the enemy unopposed, and carry one thousand disciplined soldiers into the ranks of rebellion.

At last, I settled it in this way.    The artillery and cavalry were sent over first in two voyages ; and when the boats returned the third time, I appointed one to every company of infantry, faithful and unfaithful, at intervals along the bank ; and told all to step into their respective boats at the first sound of a bugle, and at the second to push off and proceed.

This was done, but not without considerable excitement, which was now becoming irrepressible, as the enemy was known to be within a few miles ; and when at last a Poorbecuh and Sikh soldier drew their swords on each other, and the rest of their comrades were beginning to run together to the point, I thought all our pains were about to be thrown away at the last moment; but on my seizing both the combatants by the collar, and thrusting them into my own boat, and then ordering the bugler to sound for embarkation, the crowd broke sulkily up again, and got on board. Again the bugle rang out over the Indus; to my irrepressible joy every boat pushed off, and we crossed that broad river in almost as perfect a military formation as a regiment in open column of company taking ground to its left at a review.

Once on the right bank, I felt a match for the traitors; and as soon as all had disembarked, I called up the grey-headed adjutant of the Poor-beeuhs, and put the boats under the charge of him and his men. "Take them," I said, "out of the main stream two miles up the branch that leads to Dera Futteh Khan; anchor them at the back of the island, and defend them with your lives against any one who attempts to take them from you."

Moolraj's army marched into Leia at the same time that we landed on the opposite bank, and threw out a reconnoitring party to the Indus without delay, to ascertain our position, and, if possible, secure some boats; but neither were to be seen. In the course of the day, however, as I afterwards learnt, an ambassador from their camp managed to make his way over to mine, and deliver two or three pairs of gold bracelets, which Moolraj had sent to officers of the Futteh Pultun. This of course was unknown to me; but there was quite enough of disaffection apparent among the Sikh soldiers to make me very anxious for General Cortlandt's arrival with the reinforcements.

He could not now be far off; and my attempt to make out his exact distance produced one of the most striking incidents I ever witnessed.

It was a custom of Sikh armies, when they wished to proclaim their own position to an ally, or ascertain his, to fire two guns as soon as all was still at nightfall, to which the ally immediately replied, if he was within hearing.

This was well known to me, and I determined to try it on the night of 3rd May. About nine p.m., therefore, our two horse artillery guns were fired, and I bent an attentive ear for the response.

Scarcely had the echo died away, when eight guns and countless camel-swivels and muskets rent the air with their discharge; but not in the desired direction. It was the defiance of the enemy at Leia, who maintained it with successive rounds for an hour.

Such a roar of hostile artillery, in the dead of night, made a powerful impression on our little camp; and, when it ceased, dismay had fallen on many a faithful heart, when—hark!—due north there rolls down the Indus the deep boom of a distant gun;—a minute's pause, and then another boom is heard. It is the answer to our signal—heard and understood alike in those two hostile camps, divided by the Indus. *We* knew that our friends had come, and *they* that their opportunity was gone.

The long interval of an hour, which occurred between my signal and General Cortlandt's reply, and which the enemy so efficiently filled up, was afterwards thus explained. Our two guns were heard by the General's fleet, while still floating down the river; and they had to pull to the nearest shore, and disembark a gun, before they could fire in reply.

By seven o'clock next morning, the reinforcing fleet of twenty-six boats anchored alongside our camp, bringing the General, with Soobhan Khan's infantry regiment of Mohammedans, and six horse-artillery guns. General Cortlandt brought this detachment from Bunnoo in the extraordinarily short period of eight days, having marched to Dera Ishmael Khan, and thence taken boat.

None saw clearer than he to what end these events were tending; none knew better the value of every hour.

The following note by Lady Edwardes explains in few words all that is likely to have embarrassed the reader in the foregoing chapter. I know so much less of Indian matters than most Englishmen that I shrink from encumbering the pages with elucidations useless except to myself. " The ' Khálsa ' was the military body formed by Govindh Singh, the tenth Gooroo, purposely with the object of resisting the Mohammedans. The Sikhs had previously not been a warlike sect. Gooroo Nánuck, the founder, was a man of mild, unwarlike precepts. Gooroo Govindh changed the whole, and established the Khálsa, a distinctly warlike body, with significant watchwords, implying readiness for action. The Khálsa looked to their Gooroo, but otherwise were equal among themselves, and carried on their affairs by councils. This system passed into the army established and drilled by foreign European officers; and when the soldiery got the upper hand, the chief men in the regiments banded together and ruled the whole body, and showed great power, which made them afterwards so dangerous and difficult to deal with, as in our two (first and second) ' Sikh Wars ' in the Punjáb. Cortlandt was one of these foreign European officers *in the service of the Sikhs,* when he first came upon the scenes at Bunnoo, and joined with Herbert."

END OF PART II.

# PART III.

## THE PATIENCE OF KINEYREE.

---

## CHAPTER I.

### *INQUISITIVE.*

ALTHOUGH in the abstract here made of Lieutenant Edwardes' diary, I have been compelled to omit many passages far more clearly explanatory of his personal character than those collated, thus fragmentarily, to mark the course of events, I believe the thoughtful reader cannot but already feel the many reasons I had for calling him a missionary more than a soldier—though a consummate soldier to begin with. The general public is apt to estimate victory by its cost, and success, as now everything else, by its visible magnitude. Whereas, in right estimate of battle gift in chiefs, the victories are greatest which are conclusive in result, because the blow is struck at the right time; and only the success true, which is secure because it is just.

If I am spared to continue 'Prӕterita,' its

readers will find, what I think they would hardly have guessed from my general writings, that I have been a constant and careful student of battles, from the time when I first began to invent them geometrically on known dispositions of ground for my own pleasure. And in the range from Marathon to Inkermann, I know not another instance of generalship, under the most difficult conditions, so absolutely swift, ingenious, and permanently and beneficently successful, as these two campaigns of Edwardes in Bunnoo and the Doâb. *Beneficently* successful, securing not only the loyal attachment of conquered tribes to—I was going to have said, himself—but ought rather to say, to the English character he represented, but developing in them the most beautiful charities, and understandings of each other, as in the case of the returning outlaw under Shah Niwaz of Tâk.

The general points respecting battle tenor and conduct which I had gathered from my mixed reading were intended to have been enforced in an abstract of the battles of Friedrich, which I had in preparation when Carlyle's too swift death took away all my heart for it. The great difficulties in such work are, first, to rescue from exaggeration what the battle really was; and, secondly, from the lucky or unlucky accidents of the fact, what it was *meant* to be, when either general has a meaning at all. At Alma, Lord Raglan, losing his way, finds himself with his staff, on a sudden, in the middle of the Russian lines. He observes to his surprised suite, "Our presence here will be of the greatest advantage." It was so ; but it was not an advantage Lord Raglan had calculated on. And the battle was won, not by Lord Raglan, but by Colonel Yea and Sir Colin Campbell.

Too many of our English victories, (we are in the extremely bad habit of forgetting our defeats,) have been of this accidental character, their blunders redeemed by hard fighting and cruel loss. On the other hand, all Friedrich's battles are composed with the precision of a musical arrangement. When he fails, it is either because his orders have been disobeyed, or because difficulties occur in their execution which no foresight could have anticipated. The only quite sound and flawless fulfilments of his orders are at Leuthen, Rossbach, and Sohr.* Kolin was lost by the direct disobedience of a general officer ; Kunersdorf by the unexpected strength

* Sohr is the most interesting of all. "He himself gallops to the piquet on the heights, glass in hand. 'Austrian army, sure enough, thirty to thirty-five thousand of them,—we only eighteen.' Friedrich gallops down, with his plan clear enough ; and already the Austrians, horse and foot, are deploying upon the heights he has quitted."

of a fort, which could not have been previously estimated ; and Torgau cost dearer than a defeat, by the inconceivable misunderstanding of Ziethen. Curiously, Hohenfriedberg, the most cunningly and long in advance prepared of all his battles, is thrown into some confusion by accident of ground, causing delay in movement ; and the brilliancy of its success is finally owing to the refusal of Gessler to receive the king's consequent order conveyed to him by Valori, and remaining doggedly where the king himself had told him to stay.

It is especially also to be noticed that Fried-rich's battles are all passionate. He loses his head in defeat, rides away out of the first sight of it at Mollwitz, protracts the ruin of Kolin in desperation, and would fain have fallen by a chance bullet at Kunersdorf. The Duke of Wellington is totally the contrary of him in this particular. His battles are the severe application of perfect military science, with perfect coolness of nerve, absolutely conquered passion, (such passion as he had to conquer,) a certain quantity always of the best soldier material in the world to work with, (Irish and Scotch,) * with admirable staff officers for his

* " It was a Highland rear-lorn hope that covered the broken wreck of Cumberland's army after the disastrous day of Fontenoy, when more British soldiers lay dead upon the field than fell at Waterloo itself. It was another Highland regiment that scaled

friends, and usually second- or third-rate ones for his enemies. Until 1815, he had never met one good general except Massena ;—over whom he gained no advantage. But he never makes a mistake, never neglects a detail, never falls into a trap, and never misses an opportunity. Also, when he sees that a thing *can* be done, he does it, without asking how many men it will cost. It will for ever remain a question between the two nations whether Waterloo was lost by Napoleon's misuse of his cavalry, or Wellington's discipline of his infantry. But there is no

the rock face over the St. Lawrence, and first formed a line in the September dawn on the level sward of Abraham. It was a Highland line that broke the power of the Maharatta hordes, and gave Wellington his maiden victory at Assaye. Thirty-four battalions marched from these glens to fight in America, Germany, and India, ere the eighteenth century had run its course. And yet while, abroad over the earth, Highlanders were thus first in assault and last in retreat, their lowly homes in far-away glens were being dragged down ; and the wail of women and the cry of children went out upon the same breeze that bore too upon its wings the scent of heather, the freshness of gorse blossom, and the myriad sweets that made the lowly life of Scotland's peasantry blest with health and happiness.

"There are crimes done in the dark hours of strife, and amid the blaze of man's passions, that sometimes make the blood run cold as we read of them ; but they are not so terrible in their red-handed vengeance as the cold malignity of a civilised law which permits a brave and noble race to disappear by the operation of its legalised injustice." (Colonel Butler, in ' Far-out Rovings Retold.')

question at all that a general of the highest
quality,—Friedrich, Black Edward, or Castruccio
de' Castracani,—with the entire force of Prussia
and England at his command, would have crushed
Napoleon without losing ten thousand men in a
single day.

But there is one military character in which
Friedrich, Napoleon, Wellington, and Nelson, all
are alike.    They, and the men they command,
and the nations they represent, alike *hate their
enemies.*    England  and  France  mean,  in  war,
nothing  but  mischief  to  each  other ;  so,  alas,
Prussia and Austria,—France and Prussia.    In all
battles  commanded  by  these  generals,  they  lead
men in whom they can entirely trust, against men
to whom they mean no mercy.

The  character  of  the  missionary  soldier  whose
campaign  we  are  studying,  no  less  than  his
circumstances,  are  the  absolute  reverse.    He  had
not  a  single  man  of  his  own  nation,  or  religion,
under  his  command ;  while  among  his  enemies
there  are  many  to  whom  he  wishes  only  good,
there  are  none  to  whom  he  wishes  evil.    He  is
continually striving to spare life on both sides, on
all  sides—not  only  to  spare,  but  to  educate,  to
convince,  and  to  win.    With  whomsoever  he  deals,
his  first  dealing  is  absolute  justice.    " They  sent

him with an escort—*I* put him in irons." Then,
what good or virtue is in them he will seize and
cherish ;—of nearly all material he makes something,—of the best, everything ; he has the loyalest
and the most various friends, and even the men
who dread him most, partly love him through
their fear. " What shall we do with this Sahib of
ours ? " There would have been no question what
was to be done with any other Sahib at such
a time.

I leave to his much-loved wife the privilege
of giving the history of his religious feelings
and faith, so far as they regulated his own
life and were the foundation of its happiness.
The sense in which I have used the word
" Faith " in the text and the name of this book,
is that of trust not only in the protection of
God, but in the nobleness and kindness of men.
The complete record which I believe Lady
Edwardes may be able to place before the
public, before, perhaps, the first sheet of this
broken sketch can be in their hands, will contain,
I doubt not, the most singular instances of the
fearless power given him by this conviction, on
the most critical occasions, and under the most
difficult conditions. Let us pass now to the
conclusion of our own tale.

# CHAPTER II.

I AM obliged to omit all official, and many material, details, in this part of the story; and must sum the effective state of things as I best can, to enable the reader to understand the sequel.

The British Governor-General and Commander-in-Chief agreeing that British soldiers cannot march in warm weather, the Resident at Lahore writes to Lieutenant Edwardes that he is to stay where he is—on the west side of Indus; —and that he is quite strong enough to hold his own there, and keep Moolraj on the other side for the present; and that Moolraj shall be presently shut up in Mooltan by five converging arrangements, and no harm come to him, or of him, for six months, and then he shall be besieged in form, and taken, and sate upon, &c., &c.

Of course Lieutenant Edwardes cannot contradict his commander-in-chief; but takes the liberty to explain to the Resident that until Moolraj *is* shut up by the converging arrangements, it will not be easy to guard a hundred miles' length of ferriable river against him, night and day; and also, that if the murder of two British officers, and rebellion of a Sikh city is left unnoticed for six months, there may be other Sikhs, not to say Bunnoochees and Afghans, who may take to haymaking in a similar style during the warm weather; but that if, at once, *one* of the five arrangements can be carried out—that is to say, the Dâoodpotras of the well-disposed Bhawul Khan moved against Moolraj from the south, and he himself be allowed to cross Indus and go in with them at Moolraj as hard as he can hit,—he will answer for the good end of the whole matter.

On this representation follows a fortnight of official correspondence,—most of it lost, with the postbags, to Moolraj's rough riders; during which time Edwardes and General Cortlandt, between them, guard Indus as best they may. But at last Bhawul Khan's men are really got to move on Mooltan; and then Lieutenant Edwardes—having quite properly asked leave to cross Indus himself—though he has not got it, assumes, with every appearance of probability, that it was in the missing postbags, and crosses Indus accordingly; meekly advising the Resident, of course, that he has done so. On which he gets forbidden, still more strictly, to cross the Chenab, still between him and Mooltan, which accordingly he very obediently does not—but only moves quite up to the edge of it, and sits down to look at it. Whereupon——

If the reader will now set open the map on page 143, and refer carefully to it through the rest of this chapter, he will, I think, have no further difficulty in following, through the entries of Sir Herbert's diary, the more detailed manner of their happening, in the events I have thus shortly fore-sketched; and the practical issues of all these arrangements, through the succeeding chapters. Which commence thus:—

"ONE of the first duties which I intrusted to General Cortlandt, after his joining me at Dera Futteh Khan, was that of thoroughly ascertaining the condition of the suspected Futteh Pultun. This his long familiarity with Sikh soldiers would enable him to do much better than I could: he had Sikh orderlies attached to him, who could worm any secret out of their countrymen; and he had above all an honourable partiality for the Sikh army, in which he had served so many years, which would make him glad to exculpate the regiment if he could, and correct my own prejudices against them.

The General was fully alive to the importance of an inquiry on which the safety of the whole camp might any day depend ; and spared no pains to ascertain the truth.

In particular, his Sikh orderlies had leave to spend the day with their friends in the Sikh regiment ; and under the genial influence of a full stomach, the brightly dawning prospects of the Khalsa nation, the ability displayed by the Sikh garrison of Mooltan in making Moolraj's ambition a tool to embroil the British in another war,—the bold manifesto they had sent to the Futteh Pultun at Leia, how the Futteh Pultun hailed it, and sent off deputies to Mooltan to sell their services,—the rewards Moolraj had held out in reply,—the heavy gold bangles he had clinked and jingled in their ears,—the dispatch of a rebel force against us to bring things to a crisis,—my untimely suspicions and retreat,—all these topics were unreservedly canvassed : and such a thoroughly treacherous and disaffected spirit displayed, such a greedy looking forward to the coming revolution with its plunder and rewards, that the spies summed up their report to the General in the evening with the emphatic figure, "that the mouths of the Futteh Pultun were as wide open as they could go, and would swallow anything."

This being the alarming state of the Sikhs in our own camp, we next sent over spies to that of the enemy at Leia.

They returned in the evening of May 5th, and reported the rebel force to consist of four infantry regiments (among them the Ghoorkhas who deserted Agnew and Anderson), two thousand Puthán, and one thousand Sikh and Punjábee cavalry, eight horse-artillery guns, two heavy ditto, sixty camel-swivels, and two more heavy guns coming up from the rear;—in fact, almost the whole of Moolraj's disposable force at that time, and under the command of his brother, Shám Sing.

Having myself no letters as yet from the Resident, I was obliged to draw conclusions from the movements of the enemy.

It was clear that he had neither news of an army coming against him from Lahore, nor expectation of one being sent, else he dared not have thrown all his strength across the Chenab, to oppose a single British officer with a mere detachment. I could only conjecture, therefore, that the season was declared too far advanced for a British army to take the field ; that the Resident thought a Sikh army would be worse than none; and that consequently no operations would be undertaken against Mooltan during the hot season.

Should that course be adopted, Moolraj would be at liberty, for some months, to turn his arms in whatever direction he chose; and the force he had already dispatched to Leia showed his decided predilection for destroying *me*.

Looking round me for the means of meeting such a campaign, I saw clearly that, exert myself as I might in the enlistment of the border tribes, I never could keep them together in sufficient numbers to perform the double office of overawing doubtful friends and fighting open enemies, without a large exchequer.

Old soldiers, and loyal soldiers, don't like fighting long without pay; but mercenaries will not fight at all.

Where was I to get money from? The revenues of General Cortlandt's province were insufficient to pay the Sikh troops already in it; and the treasury at Lahore was emptied by the ordinary expenses of the State as fast as revenues came in. There was not room for another drummer-boy's fist in the Sikh military-chest.

One way alone was open to me to get money, and that was to take it from Moolraj; to defend my own provinces by taking *his*, and feed my own soldiers out of the revenues of the country they could wrest from *him*.

I thought this feasible, if I could get an ally to help me, if only by distracting the enemy's attention ; and, on the 5th of May, I wrote to ask the Resident for the assistance of Bháwul Khan, the Nuwab of Bhawulpoor, a Mohammedan * Prince, whose territory was only divided from that of Mooltan by the Sutlej, and whose character for fidelity to the British Government stood high.

If not, I begged him to send me no more Sikhs !

On the 6th of May, the rapid rising of the Indus threatened soon to overwhelm us, unless we moved away from the margin of its banks ; and I reconnoitred the country for a better spot to encamp in. The country people showed me one in the direction of the fort of Girâng ; but I feared the moral effect of a retrograde movement, however small, and determined to move to the front, if it were only a mile (*i.e.*, south, towards Mooltan).

On the 7th of May, however, there was another

---

* In the first part, this prince is erroneously described as a Hindū. I took him for one because he sent a stupid commander with his force, instead of leading it himself ; and I never cared enough about him to make him out. The reader will find all that I have said of the differences between the two religions entirely sound, whatever mistakes I may have made in particular instances.

shifting of the scenes.  The rebel army broke up from Leia, and retreated with such precipitation that all discipline was lost.  Moolraj's orders to his brother were " to make Mooltan in two marches,"—a feat just possible, the distance being seventy miles, with a broad river to cross.

Many reasons were given out by the rebels for this move ; but believing that it could only be to defend Mooltan from some of our approaching armies, I once more crossed a picket of one hundred horsemen over the Indus to Leia, to gain intelligence for our future guidance.  Whereupon Moolraj's Governor once more abandoned his government, and fled with his guards, leaving some artillery horses and other impediments behind him, and the picket took peaceful possession of the city.

On the 8th of May I received a letter from the Resident, dated April 29th !  It informed me that he approved of all I had done, and had written to me constant letters (none of which I had received), containing full instructions (of which I was consequently ignorant).

Later in the day a second letter-bag came in, (the communication being no longer intercepted by the enemy).  It contained only a short note ; but this conveyed the Resident's explicit instructions to keep to the right bank of the river, protect my own province, and do all in my power to secure the fidelity of the regular troops with me. This last I had already done, by enlisting Putháns to over-awe them ; and with reference to the two former points, so long as our main body was trans-Indus, no danger and many advantages could arise from keeping a picket at Leia.*

A still more urgent communication next came in. It was from Moolraj's right-hand man, Moostapha Khan, Khághwánee, who had come in one day all the way from Mooltan to Sooltán Kee Kote, twelve miles from Leia, to deliver a message from his master, and requested my right-hand man, Foujdar Khan, to meet him and receive it. Foujdar was of opinion that the ambassador was too honourable a man to leave Moolraj without his consent, and too useful to be sent on any but the most important business. So I sent Foujdar Khan off in a boat, full of trusty followers, to float down the Indus to the ferry nearest Sooltán Kee Kote, and ordered him on no account to land in the enemy's country ; but send word to Moostapha Khan that he might come down to the river if he had anything to say.

My impression was that Moolraj had thoughts of

* The reader will doubtless observe Master Herbert's philosophical way of doing as he is bid.

surrender; so I not only complied with his ambassador's request, but wrote a few lines of invitation to Moostapha Khan to come to my own camp, if he had anything of importance to communicate to me.

He accepted the invitation, and returned next day with Foujdar Khan.

His commission was a fair specimen of Oriental diplomacy. It consisted of two parts: one public, the other private.

The private instructions were to buy over Foujdar Khan, whose utility to me made him obnoxious to the rebels.

The public orders were to inquire if I had authority to treat with Moolraj; and if so, what assurances I could give him if he surrendered?

To the latter I replied, that neither I, nor the Resident at Lahore, nor any one else, had authority to stand between the murderer of the two British officers and the retributive justice which their countrymen would demand.

Moostapha Khan met this by warmly defending his master from the guilt of that cowardly deed, and said that all Moolraj demanded was "justice and a fair trial." This he repeated so often and earnestly, that I really believed Moolraj's heart misgave him, and that he was seriously entertaining

15

the design of coming in, and throwing all the blame upon his soldiers. I did not believe that in a court of justice he could ever establish his innocence to the satisfaction of any one of common sense ; but if he wished for the opportunity, I conceived it to be my duty to assure him that a fair trial in a British court of justice would be granted him at any time, and both life and honour be safe if he were pronounced not guilty.

Public business being thus transacted, the envoy turned to his private memoranda.

He had ascertained, on the road, that Foujdar Khan was not " for sale " at present, having already found a purchaser, with whose chances of ultimate success he was well content. Moreover, Foujdar managed to convince him that it would be a much better stroke of business to sell himself, and the rest of their mutual countrymen, the Puthán officers of Moolraj's garrison.

To do Moostapha Khan and his Puthán friends justice, they had little heart in their master's rebellion ; some of them (among whom was Moostapha) had even refused to set their seals to the oath of allegiance in such a cause ; and all would have gladly seen the affair brought to a termination.

What they most ardently desired was, if possible, to induce the Dewan to surrender ; in which case

they would have surrendered with him, and their
honour and fidelity as soldiers remained free from
stain.    But if this could not be brought about,
then they were generally resolved to separate
themselves from Moolraj, but not to act on the
side of the Maharajah and the British.

Moostapha Khan, therefore, now acted on what
he knew to be the secret plans of his countrymen
in Mooltan.   He had secured a written promise of
a fair trial for Moolraj, and would use it on his
return to the Dewan as a new argument for surrender.    But he had in his own mind little expectation of success, and turned with greater earnestness
to the alternative.

Before entering into any negotiation with the
Puthán portion of the Mooltan garrison, I thought
it only right to ascertain distinctly what share they
had taken in the murder of my own countrymen.
For as yet I only knew, by common report, that
the Putháns were the anti-war, and the Sikhs and
Poorbceuhs the war party.

Moostapha Khan declared that the rebellion from
beginning to end was the work of Hindūs ; that
of the two miscreants who first attacked Agnew
and Anderson, one was a Dogruh, and the other
a Sikh ; and that all the subsequent events, and
the readiness with which the Lahore escort sided

with the Mooltan soldiery, were viewed with regret by the majority at least of the Puthán officers in Moolraj's service. Mr. Agnew had spoken kindly to them all, and assured them of employment under the Crown ; so that they were certain of an honourable maintenance, and had nothing to gain by retaining the Dewan in power; while, on the other hand, they had lately been estranged from him by his ceasing to intrust them with the chief management of his affairs, and choosing for his favourites and counsellors men of vulgar birth, whose airs and slights had become insufferable.

In short, he said, whether they receive encouragement or not from you, the Puthán officers are prepared to quit Moolraj if he persists in the rebellion ; they have already removed their wives and children out of Mooltan to a fort of our own, named Kummur Kote, twenty koss south-east of Mooltan ; and our only object in now informing you beforehand is to record the motives on which we act, and establish our future claim to employment.

I received the above account at the time with more suspicion than I now know it deserved, for I felt strongly that nothing could justify even the passive adherence of the Puthán officers to their rebellious master ; but on the whole it convinced me that the guilt of our countrymen's blood was upon the Sikh and Hindū portion of the garrison, and that the Puthāns had contributed no more towards the rebellion than they could now counter-balance by their defection.

Accordingly, I closed with the envoy's offer, and guaranteed an honourable maintenance to all the Puthāns who should desert Moolraj and withdraw to Kummur Kote, on this condition—that they were innocent of the blood of Agnew and Anderson.

Moostapha Khan, therefore, returned to Mooltan with two guarantees in his pocket.

A guarantee to Moolraj of a fair trial before a British court of justice, if he felt innocent enough to surrender.

And a guarantee of employment under the Crown to all the Puthán officers who, having hands un-stained with British blood, chose to go no farther with Dewan Moolraj.

How ultimately the breach between the Dewan and his Puthán officers so widened, that they not only left him, but fought on my side against him, will be related in due course ; but I may as well close the other point here.

The ambassador himself had no expectation of the Dewan's surrender ; for with true Afghan sar-casm he had said to me at parting, " Moolraj has asked for a fair trial, but he will hardly accept it. After all, what is he? A Hindū! And did you ever know a Hindū who had the magnanimity to throw himself on the honour of an enemy? His very fears have made him desperate; and he will scarcely give himself up alive." *

* The speech was justified to every letter, except the last. Moolraj had more confidence in his military resources than in his innocence ; and chose the plain and the fortress before the prison and the dock. Timid by nature, and untrained to arms, his circumstances of mingled danger and temptation created in him every kind of courage. except the personal—in every degree except the last and rarest. He found, if he possessed it not before, the courage to dare the British power, the courage to murder its magistrates. the courage to hope to be a king, the courage to direct military operations, and the courage to endure and protract a siege ; but he neither had, nor found, the courage to run the risk of a wound in saving the lives of two innocent men ; he had not the courage to fly and throw himself on the mercy of the power he had unwillingly outraged ; he had not the courage to lead his own army in the battles to which. with taunts, he urged them on ; and he had not the courage at last to die, like Mozuffur Khan, in the breach of his battered fortress, and throw the pall of glory over his buried crimes.

He *did* 'give himself up alive.' He was brought to trial; found guilty; sentenced to death; mercifully reprieved, and transported. In short, he lived to ascertain what would have been, at worst, his fate had he surrendered, under my guarantee, before the war. I forbear from conjecturing whether his cell is darkened by the reflection that his not doing so cost many thousands of brave men their lives, and his own Sovereign a throne; but on our side it must ever remain a subject of satisfaction that he was not denied the 'justice in open court' which he first sought, and then refused. On Moolraj alone rests the awful responsibility of the war which followed.

# CHAPTER III.

*" Lieutenant Edwardes to the Resident.*

" Camp, Gaggianwallah Ferry, *on the right bank of the Chenab* "
[italics mine—he has not yet crossed it ; but only 'looked
at it,' till he thinks he had better], "nine koss south of
Khángurh and Shoojabád, June 17th, 1848."

" I HAVE to thank you for the confidence you
repose in me, in leaving me 'unfettered, to
act according as circumstances render it most
expedient that I should, for the purpose of
obtaining the great object in view ' * ; without
this, indeed, my position would, be still more
difficult than it is, and the army I have enlisted
be reduced to inutility. The operation now going
on is a good illustration : Dewan Moolraj has
concentrated his whole force, for one decisive
effort against the Dàoodpotra army, east of the
Chenab, with the avowed intention of destroying
that army and mine, successively and separately,
and so ridding himself of the only enemies he

* Wrong, Master Herbert. You had no business to express anything but your thanks to Sir Frederick ; you should not have quoted
his own twaddle to him. (J. R.)

sees in the field. It is quite possible that the Dâoodpotra army (which, by my advice, has in the course of the last two days strengthened itself, by calling in its detachments west of the Chenab and south-east of Mooltan) would be equal to encountering the Moolraj troops ; but they evidently were not of that opinion themselves, and repeatedly called on me to come to their assistance. The impolicy also of leaving them to run the risk was sufficiently obvious, when the event could be made certain by junction ; yet I had no authority from you to cross the Chenab, and only a reluctant permission to cross the Indus under pressing emergency.

"In resolving to follow the Koreyshee army across the Chenab, and unite with Bháwul Khan's troops, I have been obliged to incur the, at all times, dangerous responsibility to a political officer, of acting contrary to orders ; * and it is a relief to me, on the very bank of the forbidden river, to receive your kind and considerate *carte blanche.*

"I am happy to inform you that the heavy firing heard by us at Khangurh yesterday morning,

---

* Yes; but you needn't have said so; and Sir Frederick could then have left everybody to suppose you didn't, and that all the credit of the affair was his. I don't say he would; but your book would have been better received at Knightsbridge. (J. R.)

in the direction of the Dâoodpotra camp, turned
out not to be an engagement with the enemy,
but a prolonged *feu-de-joie* of artillery, on hearing
of our rapid approach to their assistance.

"Dewan Moolraj's force, under Lalla Rung
Rám, is still encamped within two koss* to the
south of Shoojabád, taking up a strong position,
it is supposed to await our united arrival, instead
of hurrying on a collision this morning, as
positively ordered, with the Dâoodpotras before I
could come up.  This is a fatal error, as, please
God, they will find.  The rebel movements show
occasional flashes of military skill and enterprise
in their design, but they invariably fade away
when it comes to execution, and end in a weak
retreat.

"The Dâoodpotras are still at Goweyn, twelve
koss from Shoojabád, where they have wisely
intrenched themselves till our arrival.

"General Cortlandt, with the guns and regular
troops, joined me yesterday, at Klángurh ; and as
soon as the moon rose, the march was again
resumed to this place, between nine and ten koss† ;
even this distance is a great effort in this severe
heat.  The Dâoodpotras are sending us up forty-
seven boats, in which Moozooddeen Khan crossed

---

* Three and one-eighth miles.          † Fifteen miles.

his detachment yesterday. They will be here in a few hours, when the passage of the Chenab will immediately commence. Our numbers have swelled to nearly nine thousand men, and I am afraid we shall not be all over under three days ; I have left it to Futteh Mohammed Khan, Ghorce, to fix the point of junction.

"When our two forces unite, we shall not be under eighteen thousand men, twenty-one guns, and about fifty zumbooruhs ; and I cannot conceive the enemy awaiting such a force at Shoojabád. Even in intrenchments, natives look to numbers, and the rebels have got neither the consciousness of honesty, nor the prestige of success, to support them.

"Were the Sikh troops on the frontier to be relied on for a moment, I would at this juncture make a rush at Mooltan, and, leaving Rung Rám in his intrenchment, get between him and his master, who is left, with a few personal guards only, in the fort.

"But the struggle now going on is of such a mixed nature, that the step would probably be unsuccessful ; Moolraj is chief of the rebellion, merely by the accident of holding the *moshuksah* (lease, or contract, of the revenues) of Mooltan. The Sikhs have not espoused his cause out of attachment to him, but because it holds out an opportunity of renewing the old Khalsa struggle. It would therefore annoy them but little to separate Moolraj from the rebel army; they would probably abandon him to his fate, cross the Chenab, join Jhunda Singh's force at Leia, and call on those at Bunnoo and Peshawur to rise at once, in the name of the Khalsa. We should quell a rebellion, and get an insurrection in its stead.* I shall bend all my efforts, therefore, to driving the rebels into Mooltan, if we cannot bring them to an engagement in the plain.

"The force beyond Leia is a source of considerable anxiety to me; the majority of the Churunjeet regiment has joined Juss Müll,† Dewan Moolraj's Kárdár at that place; and it is but too apparent that the guns of Úmeer Chund and Dhara Singh's infantry regiment are inclined to join them. Your orders are, to send Jhunda

---

* The distinction is a little too subtle in terms so short. He means, of course, by a 'rebellion,' the disobedience of a few rebellious persons to an established government; by 'insurrection,' the resolution of a nation to change its government—if it can.

† Sir Herbert's lovely book was made nearly unreadable, at the time, by these unlucky Jeets and Jusses and Mulls. He had no time to weed it of them.—The reader will have sense to see the difference between my revision in such points of my friend's rapid work, and the mastication by vile publishers of Scott's and other great men's deliberate work, for the mob's maw, and their own profit.

Singh's force to Jhung—most probably to avoid this very catastrophe; and I have forwarded the order to Jhunda Singh; *but I have also told him not to act upon it,** if he thinks it would only make the men declare themselves, and go openly over to Moolraj. The Churunjeet regiment were led to decide for Moolraj, by Jowáhir Mull trying to get rid of them, by sending them on a frivolous excuse to Pind Dadun Khan. Seeing that they were suspected, they threw away the mask, and instead of marching on Pind Dadun Khan, bent their steps to Leia. It is a serious addition to our difficulties, thus to find our allies turning enemies, but there is no help for it; all we can do, is to increase our efforts to shut Moolraj up in Mooltan, and thus discourage all his friends.

"Your appointment of Lieutenant Lake to the political charge of the Bhawulpoor force is both timely and happy.

"That officer's personal courage, and professional talent, will find a field prepared for them."

---

* Italics mine. The 'rider' is very characteristic of Sir Herbert's combined audacity and subtlety. The Duke would have sent the order as he received it, held himself silently prepared accordingly, and lost a thousand men or so in redeeming the damage. It was his notion of 'duty'—but he always meant duty to the barracks. Sir Herbert would neither have had his windows broken by the mob, nor, if he had, put up iron shutters afterwards.

As my next letter to the Resident was written
"on the field of battle," after fighting for nine
hours under an Indian sun in June, with the
wrecks of a bloody struggle lying round me as
I sat on the ground, and as yet the details of
that struggle only imperfectly known to myself;
I shall here depart for a moment from the
general rule I have adopted of letting the "Blue
Book" tell the tale with the addition of occasional new comments and explanations; and shall
endeavour to give the reader a more full and just
idea of the battle of Kineyree.

On the day of the 17th June, the relative
strength and positions of the three armies were as
follows:—The rebel army, of from eight thousand
to ten thousand horse and foot, and ten guns,
commanded by Moolraj's brother-in-law, Rung
Rám, and the Dâoodpotra army of about eight
thousand five hundred horse and foot, eleven
guns and thirty zumbooruhs, commanded by
Futteh Mohammed Khan, Ghoree, were on the
left bank of the Chenab; and my force, consisting
of two divisions (one of faithful regulars, foot
and artillery, of the Sikh service, about one thousand five hundred men, and ten guns, under
General Cortlandt, and another of about five
thousand irregulars, horse and foot, and thirty

zumbooruhs, under my own personal command), was upon the right bank.*

Rung Rám's camp was pitched across the high road to Mooltan, three miles south of Shoojabád; Futteh Mohammed's at Goweyn, fifteen miles farther south; and mine at Gaggianwallah Ferry, about twelve miles south of Khángurh.

The three formed a triangle; in which the Dâoodpotras were nearer to me than to the enemy, but nearer to the enemy than I was; while a river about three miles wide divided the allies.

It is obvious that, in such a position of affairs, had Rung Rám marched upon the Dâoodpotras on the morning of the 17th, his numbers being equal, if not superior, and his *matériel* far better, (Moolraj's soldiers being chiefly experienced regulars, and Bhâwul Khan's chiefly irregulars who had never seen a round shot fired,) he must have defeated my allies before I could get across the river, and perhaps have prevented me from crossing at all.

That he did not do this, I attribute partly to the divided councils of a native camp, but chiefly to Rung Rám's uncertainty as to my

_____

* In all, fifteen thousand men (not eighteen thousand as he had hoped), twenty-one guns, and sixty zoombooruhs.

intentions. He was afraid I should cross the Chenab above him at Khángurh; and he had no wish to be placed between two fires.

About noon on the 17th, he obtained correct information that I had moved south to Gaggian-wallah, and was endeavouring to effect a junction with the Dâoodpotras. But it was too late to march fifteen miles to Goweyn, and fight a battle with Futteh Mohammed before night. So Rung Rám waited till the evening, and then moved eight miles lower down the Chenab, to the village of Bukree, which brought him within an easy march of Kincyree, where he knew I must cross from Gaggianwallah; and he calculated on occupying Kineyree early the next morning, and so keeping me on the right bank while he thrashed the Dâoodpotras on the left.

The merit of defeating this plan is due to Peer Ibraheem Khan, Buhadoor, the Native Political Agent of the British Government at the Court of Bhawulpoor.

This able and faithful officer had accompanied the Dâoodpotra army from Bhawulpoor to Goweyn, and counteracted in no small degree the imbecility of its General, Futteh Mohammed Khan.

No sooner did Rung Rám issue orders for a

move to the south on the evening of the 17th, than the Peer's spies brought him the intelligence ; and the Peer immediately sent it on to me, adding his own belief that the place where the rebels meant to halt for the night was Bukree. "Under these circumstances," said the Peer, "I would advise our moving down to Kineyree, to secure the ferry, and cover your disembarkation."

The Peer was one of those men who are found only on frontiers, as the chamois is found only amid snows. On one side of his girdle was a pen, and on the other a sword ; and he had a head, a hand, and a heart, ready to wield either with vigour.

The advice which he now gave was admirable ; and I not only adopted it, but gave him a positive order to carry it out upon the spot. "Tell Futteh Mohammed," I sent him word, "to strike his tents, and march down to this ferry at whatever hour of the night this letter reaches you ; and if he refuses, supersede him.* *It must be done*, and there is no time for correspondence." At the same time I promised, if possible, to have three thousand men and ten guns across the river to meet the Dâoodpotras on their arrival.

While this order was on its way to the Dâood-

* This is quite official : but brief ! as was needful.

potras, I held a consultation with General Cortlandt and Foujdar Khan (who by this time had
become 'Adjutant-General!' of the Puthán levies),
as to the order of our passage over the Chenab.

We had as yet but a few boats, which had been
collected for us by Moozooddeen Khan, Khághwánee, an officer of Nuwab Bháwul Khan's; and
if we attempted to pass the regular troops over
first, very few could be got over before morning;
and as to the guns, it was deemed unsafe to cross
them during the night at all. Finally, therefore,
it was resolved that the boats should be filled
choke-full of picked Irregular Infantry and dismounted cavalry, whose chief officers should be
allowed to take their horses, but no other horse
were to go till morning.

In this way a strong division of three thousand
Puthán Irregulars, with about fifty mounted chiefs,
effected the passage; *and their commander, Foujdar
Khan, boldly led them forward** in the direction
whence the Dáoodpotra column might be expected,
and met it about a mile from the river, a little
before sunrise.

* The reader cannot pay too much attention to the character of
Foujdar Khan, faultless in all relations, and fearless in all act.

# CHAPTER IV.

## *THE CHARGE OF FOUJDAR KHAN.*

I SLEPT that night on the right bank, intending to take over a second division as soon as the fleet returned from its first voyage. But at six o'clock on the 18th there was no fleet to be seen. Two little ferry-boats had, however, come up from another ferry; and, getting into these with a few horsemen and servants, and leaving General Cortlandt to pass the rest of the force over as rapidly as he could, I pushed off for Kineyree.

About a hundred yards from the left bank, I was roused from a " brown study," not unnatural amid plans so doubtful in their issue, so heavy in their responsibility, by a burst of artillery within a mile or two of the shore. A second cannonade replied, was answered, and replied again; and two tall opposite columns of white smoke rose out of the jungle, higher and higher at every discharge, as if each strove to get above its adversary, then broke and pursued each other in thick clouds over the fair and peaceful sky.

Gazing at this unmistakable symbol of the fight below, I could scarcely forbear smiling at the different speculations of my companions in the boat. The servants, men of peace, declared and hoped it was only "a salute," fired by the Dâood-potras in honour of the allies who had joined them ; but the horsemen knit their brows, and devoutly cried "Al-lah! Al-lah!" at every shot, with an emphasis like pain on the last syllable. They quite *felt* there was a fight going on.

For my own part, I felt so too ; and as I stepped on shore, and buckled the strap of my cap under my chin, I remember thinking that no Englishman could be beaten on the 18th of June.

Nor am I ashamed to remember that I be-thought me of a still happier omen, and a far more powerful aid—the goodness of my cause, and the God who defends the right. A young lieu-tenant who had seen but one campaign—alone, and without any of the means and appliances of such war as I had been apprenticed to—I was about to take command, in the midst of a battle, not only of one force whose courage I had never tried, but of another which I had never seen ; and to engage a third, of which the numbers were uncertain, with the knowledge that defeat would immeasurably extend the rebellion which I had undertaken to suppress, and embarrass the Government which I had volunteered to serve. Yet, in that great extreme, I doubted only for a moment—one of those long moments to which some angel seems to hold a microscope and show millions of things within it. It came and went between the stirrup and the saddle. It brought with it difficulties, dangers, responsibilities, and possible consequences terrible to face; but it left none behind. I knew that I was fighting for the right. I asked God to help me do my duty, and I rode on, certain that He would do it.*

On the shore, not a creature was to be seen, so we had to take the smoke and roar of the guns for our guides to the field of battle. But how to find out our own side was the difficulty, and not to fall into the hands of the enemy. On one side, the firing was regular, and apparently from guns of equal calibre; on the other side irregular and unequal, as if from guns of different sizes.

Obliged to choose between them, I paid the enemy the compliment of supposing their guns would be the best, and those of Bháwul Khan

---

* Not certain of the issue, observe; but feeling safe that, whatever the issue, his own work would be, after his prayer, the best that could be done.

the worst, and rode straight through the jungle
to the latter.

At the village of Kineyree I got a wretched
peasant to put us in the road, though he would
not go a yard along with us ; and soon we met
a horseman who had been despatched by Foujdar
Khan to tell me what had happened, and conduct
me to the field.

This was Peer Mohammed Khan, Foujdar's
uncle ; and from him I learnt that Rung Rám
had marched before dawn from Bukree to seize
the ferry at Kineyree, but finding it occupied by
my men and the Dâoodpotras, had taken up a
strong position on the salt hills of the village of
Noonár, and then opened on the allies. Hot-
tempered, brave, but ignorant of fields, and
consequently rash, the Dâoodpotra levies lifted
up their voices in one vast shout of their master's
name,* then rushed impetuously forward, without
either waiting for an order or asking for a plan.
Their very baggage was mixed up with them ;
the artillery was entangled ; and the fire which

---

* Nothing can exceed the reverence with which the Dâoodpotra
tribe regard their master, the Nuwab, or, as they call him, the
Khan. They have a most impressive custom of calling on his
name every evening, just as the sun sets below the horizon, the
whole camp joining their voices as one man. The same takes
place when they enter battle.

poured down from the heights of Noonár was so different from the matchlock volleys of their own border warfare, that they staggered, stopped, and finally fell back in a mass of confusion upon a village in their rear. Here Peer Ibraheem Khan, assisted by the oldest soldiers in the Nuwab's army, endeavoured to restore order, and persuade their General to issue the necessary commands for taking up a position, occupying the village, knocking embrasures out of the mud walls for the artillery, extricating the baggage and sending it to the rear, and, in short, putting themselves into something like an attitude of defence, since it was clear they were unable to attack.

It was at this moment that, led by Peer Mohammed, I arrived upon the field, a plain covered with jungle, amongst which loaded camels were passing to the rear, out of range of the enemy's guns, and detachments of wild-looking warriors, with red hair and beards,* were taking up a line of posts. Suddenly, a European stepped out of the crowd, and advanced to me in a hurried manner, wiping his forehead, and exclaiming, " Oh, Sir, our army is disorganized ! " —a pleasing salutation on arriving at a field of

---

* The Dâoodpotras are as fond of staining their hair red with henna, as other nations are of staining it black.

battle!    He then told me his name was Mac-
pherson, and that he commanded one of the
Nuwab's two regular regiments.    I asked him
where his General was?    He laughed, and pointed
to a large peepul-tree, round which a crowd was
gathered.    I galloped up, and looking over the
shoulders of the people, saw a little old man, in
dirty clothes, and with nothing but a skull-cap on
his head, sitting under the tree, with a rosary
in his hands, the beads of which he was rapidly
telling,* and muttering in a peevish, helpless
manner, " *Ulhumdoolilláh !    Ulhumdoolilláh !* " (God
be praised!  God be praised!) apparently quite
abstracted from the scene around him, and utterly
unconscious that six-pounder balls were going
through the branches, that officers were imploring
him for orders, and that eight or nine thousand
rebels were waiting to destroy an army of which
*he* was the General.

He had to be shaken by his people before he
could comprehend that I had arrived ; and as he
rose and tottered forward, looking vacantly in my
face, I saw that excitement † had completed the

* I am not so much of a Turk, myself, as to know how *they* use
their rosaries.  I hope the reader knows more about it.

† I say excitement, and not fear, because I have been assured
that in former years he possessed the one good quality of courage.
(Sir Herbert's own note.)

imbecility of his years, and that I might as well
talk to a post.  Turning, therefore, to the many
brave and experienced officers of his staff, and
to Peer Ibraheem Khan, who now came up, I
learnt the general nature of their position, and
then struck out a plan for the day.  "Nothing," I
said, "can be done with an army so disorganized
as this, or with guns such as Peer Ibraheem
describes yours to be.  The enemy has taken up
a strong position, and will probably prefer being
attacked.  It is not likely that he will attack
us until he thinks we don't mean to attack him.
We have therefore got the day before us.  I
will write to General Cortlandt on the other side
of the river to send us over some guns that are
better than the enemy's, and not a move must be
made till they come.  In the meanwhile, occupy
yourselves with recovering the order of your
force ; make the whole lie down in line in the
jungle ; keep them as much under cover as
possible, and let your artillery play away as
hard as they can on the enemy's guns.  Above
all, stand fast, and be patient."

The Nuwab's officers readily comprehended
what was to be done, and cheerfully promised
obedience.

I then betook myself to the left, where I

heard that my own three thousand men were posted ; and as I rode down the Dâoodpotra line, and received the loud greetings of the soldiers, I saw how timely had been my arrival. I had not joined them in a moment of triumph, but of trial. They found their ally for the first time when (in Asia at least) allies are most seldom found—in the hour of difficulty ; and seeing even a single British officer come among them to share dangers which they were encountering for the British Government, they felt its justice, and took heart again.

On reaching the left of the Dâoodpotras, I found their straggling front prolonged by my own three thousand men, who had stuck their standards upright in the turf, and were lying down in a beautiful line between them. This was the work of Foujdar Khan ; but I loudly praised all the other officers as they flocked about me.*

I now dismounted from my horse, and asked (without much hope) if any one had got pen and paper.

" Sahib ! " replied a well-known voice behind me ; and turning, I beheld Sudda Sookh,† the

---

* See his instant and subtle courtesy, and his knowledge of men. He could trust Foujdar Khan not to be jealous.

† " Sudda Sookh " was the same moonshee who taught Herbert the languages when he first went out to India and studied in order

moonshee of my office, pulling out a Cachmere pen-box and paper from his girdle, just as quietly as if he had been in cutcherry. He had no sword, or other implements of war, but merely the writing materials, with which it was his duty to be furnished ; and though he looked serious and grave, he was perfectly calm amid the roar of hostile cannon, and men's heads occasionally going off before his eyes.

"What are you doing here, Sudda Sookh?" I asked in astonishment. He put up his hands respectfully, and answered : "My place is with my master! I live by his service ; and when he dies, I die!" A more striking instance of the quiet endurance of the Hindū character I never saw.

Seating myself under a bush (in humble imitation of the Dâoodpotra General), I wrote two short notes to General Cortlandt, informing him of our critical position, and my belief that I could hold it until three p.m., by which time he must send me guns, or the battle would be lost.

These two notes I sent by two different horse-

to pass his examinations. He remained with him all the years he was in India—a most faithful and loving servant to the master he greatly honoured and respected. He was the head moonshee of his office to the last—*an honest man.* (Lady Edwardes.) This is the most beautiful example of the Hindū character which occurs during the course of events included in this book. (J. R.)

men, with an interval of half an hour between them, and the second reached the General first.

They were written at eight a.m., and what I had engaged to do was to stave off Rung Rám's army for *seven hours.* Those seven hours I should never forget if I lived seven centuries.

The firing on both sides continued for six hours without slackening ; and though the Dâood-potra artillery drew the heaviest of the enemy's fire on to the right of our line, yet my Puthláns on the left got so much more than they had ever been used to in the petty raids of their own frontier, that they were continually springing up and demanding to be led on against the enemy. " Look here," they cried, " and there, and there," (pointing to men as they were hit,) " are we to be all killed without striking a blow ? What sort of war do you call this, where there is iron on one side, and only flesh and blood on the other ? Lead us on, and let us strike a blow for our lives ! If we are to die, let us die ; but let us kill somebody first ! "

Then the officers crowded round, and every one thought he was a General ; and " if I would only listen to *him* " (pulling me by the sleeve to interrupt my rebuke to some one else), " the battle would be mine." But of all the advisers,

I must do them the justice to say, that none counselled a retreat. Every voice was for attack. Foujdar Khan, and one or two others, alone supported my opinion, that we must wait for General Cortlandt's guns. Happily, I had no doubt or misgiving in my own mind. I never had a clearer conviction in my life than I had that day that I was right, and they were wrong; and with a patience, which in the ordinary affairs of life I never had possessed, I strove hour after hour to calm that rash and excited throng, and assure them that when the proper moment should arrive, I myself would lead them on.

And so I sat out those seven hours, under a June sun, with no shade but that of a bush, and neither a drop of water nor a breath of air to lessen the intolerable heat.

A little after two p.m. the Dâoodpotras began to slacken the fire of their artillery; and, as I afterwards learnt, Futteh Mohammed, without giving me any information, and without any sort of necessity, gradually withdrew his own line, beginning with the right, and commenced falling back upon the river.

The ground we held all day was covered with jungle, which both screened and protected us so long as we lay down. No sooner, however, did the Dâoodpotras retire, than the enemy from their high post at Noonár detected the movement, and determined to follow up their advantage.

Slowly their infantry and artillery were disengaged from the village at Noonár, and their cavalry employed the interval in reconnoitring our position.

Foujdar Khan had brought across the Chenab the ten zumbooruhs which we had captured from the rebels at Leia. As yet I had not allowed these to be fired, for fear of betraying our position ; but they were now opened with effect on the reconnoitring parties of horse, who hastily fell back on the main body with the intelligence they had gained. This was about three o'clock. A short pause followed, and then the whole fire of the rebels was turned from the retiring Dâoodpotras on to the newly-discovered enemy still occupying the left.

If the wild Puthán levies had been difficult to restrain before, they were now perfectly mad, as the shot tore through their ranks and ploughed up the ground on which they lay ; and when presently the fire ceased, and bodies of horse were again seen stealing up towards our front in numbers that set our ten miserable zumbooruhs at defiance, I saw that none but the most desperate expedient could stave off the battle any longer.

Imploring the infantry to lie still yet a little longer, I ordered Foujdar Khan, and all the chiefs and officers who had horses, to mount; and forming themselves into a compact body, charge down on the rebel cavalry, and endeavour to drive them back upon the foot. " Put off the fight," I whispered to Foujdar, " or not a man of us will leave this field."

Gladly did those brave men get the word to do a deed so desperate; but with set teeth I watched them mount, and wondered how many of my choicest officers would come back.

Spreading their hands to heaven, the noble band solemnly repeated the creed of their religion, as though it were their last act on earth, then passed their hands over their beards with the haughtiness of martyrs, and drawing their swords, dashed out of the jungle into the ranks of the enemy's horse, who, taken wholly by surprise, turned round and fled, pursued by Foujdar and his companions to within a few hundred yards of the rebel line, which halted to receive its panic-stricken friends.

In executing this brilliant service, Foujdar Khan received two severe wounds, and few who returned came back untouched. Many fell.

# CHAPTER V.

## *THE GIFT OF ESAUKHEYL.*

THE purpose, however, was completely answered; for though the enemy quickly rallied, and advanced again in wrath, and I had just made up my mind that there was nothing now left but a charge of our whole line, unsupported by a single gun, of which there could have been but one result—our total annihilation—at that moment of moments might be heard the bugle-note of artillery in the rear. "Hush!" cried every voice, while each ear was strained to catch that friendly sound once more. Again it sounds—and again. The guns have come at last—thank God!

"Quick, quick, orderlies, and bring them up. There's not a moment to be lost! Now, officers, to your posts, every one to his own standard and his own men. Let the infantry stand up, and get into as good a line as the jungle will allow; let none advance until I give the word; but when the word is given, the duty of every chief is this,

—to keep the standard of his own retainers in a line with the standards right and left of him. Break the line, and you will be beaten ; keep it, and you are sure of victory."*

Away they scattered, and up sprang their shouting brotherhoods.  Standards were plucked up, and shaken in the wind ; ranks closed, swords grasped, and matches blown ; and the long line waved backwards and forwards with agitation, as it stood between the coming friend and coming foe.  Louder and louder grew the murmur of the advancing rebel host ; more distinct and clear the bugles of the friendly guns.  And now the rattling of the wheels is heard, the crack of whips, and clank of chains, as they labour to come up ; the crowd falls back, a road is cleared, we see the foremost gun, and amid shouts of welcome it gallops to the front.

Oh the thankfulness of that moment! the relief, the weight removed, the elastic bound of the heart's main-spring into its place after being pressed down for seven protracted hours of waiting for a reinforcement that might never come!  Now all is clear before us.  Our chance is nearly as good as theirs ; and who asks more ?

* This is the only manœuvre I ever attempted to instil into that impatient mass.  (Sir Herbert.)

One, two, three, four, five, *six*\* guns had come; and panting after them, with clattering cartridge-boxes, might be seen two regiments of regular infantry—Soobhan Khan's corps of Moossulmâns, and General Cortlandt's Sooruj Mookhee. It was well thought of by the General, for I had only asked for guns; but he judged well that two regiments would be worth their weight in gold at such a pinch.

There was scant time for taking breath, for the enemy was close at hand; so bidding the guns come with me, the two new regiments to follow on the guns, and the whole irregular line advance steadily in rear under command of Foujdar Khan, I led the artillery through the trees on to the cultivated plain beyond. There we first saw the enemy's line.

Directly in my front, Moolraj's regular troops were pushing their way in some confusion over fields of sugar; and through an interval of space caused by a few wells and houses, some horse artillery guns were emerging on the plain.

Round went our guns; and round went theirs; and in an instant both were discharged into each other. It was a complete surprise, for the rebels

---

\* In my despatch after the battle, I reported my own guns as ten, and those captured from the enemy as six; but we had only six of our own, and took eight—errors on the right side. (Sir Herbert.)

17

believed truly that all the guns we had in the
morning had left the field with the Dâoodpotras;
and of the arrival of the others they were
ignorant.     Down sank their whole line among
the long stalks of the sugar; and as we afterwards learnt from a Goorkha prisoner, the fatal
word was passed that the " Sahib had got across
the river with all his army from Dera Ghazee
Khan, and led them into an ambush."     To and
fro rode their astonished and vacillating Colonels;
and while the guns maintained the battle, the
intelligence was sent by swift horsemen to the
rebel General, Rung Rám, who, seated on an
elephant, looked safely down upon the fight from
the hills around the village of Noonár.

Meanwhile the Sooruj Mookhee and Soobhan
Khan's regiments had come up, followed closely
by the line; and I made the two former lie
down on the left and right of the artillery, and
the latter halt under cover of the trees.

The gunners were getting warm.     " Grape !
grape !" at length shouted the Commandant;
"it's close enough for grape;" and the enemy
thought so too, for the next round rushed over
our heads like a flight of eagles.     And there for
the first time, and the last in my short experience
of war, did I see hostile artillery *firing grape*

*into each other.* It was well for us that the enemy was taken by surprise, for they aimed high, and did little mischief. General Cortlandt's artillery were well trained and steady, and their aim was true. Two guns were quickly silenced, and the rest seemed slackening and firing wild. A happy charge might carry all. I gave the order to Soobhan Khan's regiment to attack, and away they went; Soobhan Khan himself, a stout heavy soldier, leading them on, and leaping over bushes like a boy. Before this regiment could reach the battery an incident characteristic of irregular troops occurred. A cluster of half a dozen horsemen dashed out from the trees behind me, and passing the regiment, threw themselves on the enemy's guns. Their leader received a ball full in his face, and fell over the "cannon's mouth." It was Shah Niwaz Khan of Esaukheyl.

# CHAPTER VI.

## *CONCLUSION.*

THE regiment followed, and carried at the point of the bayonet the only gun which awaited their assault. Another gun lay dismounted on the ground.

While this was doing, our guns poured grape into the cover where the rebel infantry were lying ; and these, hearing their own artillery retire before Soohban Khan's charge, retreated hastily through the high crops with which the fields were covered, but suffered heavily from the fire behind them, and formed again in great confusion when they reached their guns.

Our whole force now advanced over the contested ground, the men shouting as they passed the captured guns. The enemy then rallied, and the artillery on both sides reopened.

It was at this point of the battle that a small body of cavalry approached our battery from the left. I asked an orderly if he knew who they were ? He thought they were Foujdár Khan and the mounted chiefs of the Puthâns, and I had just turned my horse to ride towards them with an order, when a single horseman advanced, and, taking a deliberate aim, discharged a matchlock at me, within fifty or sixty yards. The ball passed first through the sleeve of the brown holland blouse which I had on, then through my shirt, and out again on the other side through both, and must have been within a hair's-breath of my elbow. But the party paid dearly for their daring, for two guns were instantly laid on them, and horses and riders were soon rolling in the dust.

And now I gave the word for the whole line of wild Puthán to be let loose upon the enemy. One volley from our battery, and they plunged into the smoke-enveloped space between the armies with a yell that had been gathering malice through hours of impatient suffering. The smoke cleared off, and the artillerymen of two more rebel guns were dying desperately at their posts, their line was in full retreat upon Noonár, and the plain was a mass of scattered skirmishes.

Once more our artillery galloped to the front, and harassed the disordered. enemy. In vain the rebels tried to rally and reply. Our infantry was on them, and another and another gun was abandoned in the flight. Rung Rám, their General, had long since fled ; Moolraj's Puthán cavalry, who had stood aloof throughout the battle, were supposed to have gone over ; the regular regiments, and especially the Goorkhas (who had deserted Agnew and Anderson at Mooltan, and now fought with halters round their necks), had borne the brunt of the day, and suffered heavily. More than half the artillery had been already lost. The pursuit was hot, and fresh and overwhelming numbers seemed to be pouring in upon both flanks ; for at this juncture the Dáoodpotras had come up again, and were burning to retrieve their place.

Thus, without a General, without order, and without hope, the rebels were driven back upon Noonár ; and having placed its sheltering heights between them and their pursuers for a moment, they threw aside shame and arms, and fled, without once halting, to Mooltan.

Few indeed would have reached that place had I had any cavalry to carry on the pursuit ; as it was, the cavalry of Nuwab Bháwul Khan maintained it for some miles, and brought in two more guns at nightfall. Out of ten that the rebels brought into the field of Kineyree, but two returned to Mooltan.

Their camp at Noonár, and all their ammunition, fell into our hands; and the former furnished many of our irregular levies with tents for the first time.

On our side, upwards of three hundred* men were killed or wounded in my own and the Nuwab's forces, and the enemy left five hundred dead upon the field.

And so ended the battle of Kineyree, which began a little after seven a.m., and was not decided till half-past four p.m.

At five p.m., after nine hours' constant exertion of mind and body, under a fiery sun, I leave the reader to imagine the feelings of thankfulness with which I sat down at Noonár, on the very ground occupied by Moolraj's army in the morning,

---

* Observe, only three hundred lost out of fifteen thousand, and the victory, total and conclusive. I did not feel it necessary to fortify with notes the assertion made above (p. 196), of the needlessness of the slaughter at Waterloo; but I have since chanced on the following passage in the account of the battle given at the time in the 'Quarterly Review,' which contains a saying of the Duke's not often quoted, and of great significance. "The Duke's aides-de-camp,—men endeared to him by their long service in the career of glory, and by their personal devotion to him,—fell, killed or wounded, one after another. At one moment, when the Duke was very far advanced, observing the enemy's movements, one of his aides-de-camp ventured to hint that he was exposing himself too much. The Duke answered, with his noble simplicity, 'I know I am, but I must die, or see what they are doing.'" This is even worse than Lord Raglan's "Our presence here will be of the greatest advantage."

and penned a hurried despatch to the Resident, announcing our victory."

There is no need to point the moral of such a story ; but of its many pointed morals, let me note these following chief arrowheads.

You have seen* a course of actions, political and military, carried out from beginning to end without a fault—without a failure, and closing in unexampled success, on all sides, and in the most difficult circumstances. But its success is not owing to Parliamentary, or any other sort of collective wisdom. It is not by a majority of votes that the Bunnoochees throw down their forts—or that the Sikhs recross the Indus—or that the Afghans abide due time of battle. In every vital moment—the Right opinion is in the minority of one !

It is not, then, by political majorities that you will get your business done well—neither is it, according to the common saying, by getting the right man in the right place. Sir Herbert fits himself for any kind of place, and is magistrate, ambassador, minister, or general, as occasion

* Hence to the close I leave the text of original lecture—addressed now, not to the good people of Coniston only, but to the British public in general.

calls. You need not think to measure the angles and the contents either of places or men. See only that you set over every business vital to you, *one* man of sense, honour, and heart.

Yet again;—you rejoice, and are proud, that your Queen, by the ministry of her brave officers, may now most truly be called Empress of India. Would it not, therefore, be well to see that she be also Empress of England: and that you are yourselves doing what the Queen would like you to do; and acting faithfully under *her* orders, instead of under the orders of the last penny print, or last absconding stockjobber?

And to close.

I do not, by any words of mine, think to deepen the impression made on you by those of the Christian hero, whose Heaven-guarded life you have to-day watched through every danger to victory. But I may tell you that the most grave personal lesson I ever received from friendship, was when Sir Herbert Edwardes read to me, in my father's house, Wordsworth's poem of the 'Happy Warrior,' and showed me that it was no symbol of imaginary character, but the practical description of what every soldier ought to be.

Such, in truth, and to the utmost, were Have-lock — Lawrence — Edwardes, — and (he himself would have added) many more of the sons of Sacred England, who went forth for her, not only conquering, and to conquer, but saving, and to save. Crusaders these indeed,—now resting all of them on their red-cross shields among the dead—but who may yet see, as the stars see in their courses, the Moabite Ruth, and the Arab Hagar, look up from their desolation to their Mother of England ; saying,—" Thy people shall be my people, and thy God, my God ! "

FINIS.

Printed by Hazell, Watson, & Viney, Ld., London and Aylesbury.

www.ingramcontent.com/pod-product-compliance
Lightning Source LLC
Chambersburg PA
CBHW031421020726

47499CB00005B/1532